MY WRONG NUMBER

A LOVE LIKE THAT NOVEL

R.L. KENDERSON

To our beta reader Leslie Michelle Hall.
She was taken from this world far too soon.
1973–2019
Thank you for all your hard work. We will miss your feedback and
support.
We know you would have liked this story.

ONE
INDY

"LISTEN, Indy, you need to just call him up, tell him to get his ass over to your house, and demand that he fuck you."

I sighed and popped a French fry in my mouth. My best friend had my best interests at heart, but things with Joel hadn't progressed to the sex stage yet.

Not because I hadn't wanted it to, but because he hadn't. At least, that was how it felt. I'd put out the signals, but he wasn't picking them up.

"I don't think that will work," I told Leslie. "We haven't even exchanged phone numbers yet."

We were having our usual after-work dinner and drinks on Friday night, and this wasn't the first time Leslie had brought up my sex life. I usually changed the subject and brushed her off, but tonight was different. I was tired of waiting for Joel to make a move and wanted her opinion.

Leslie set her beer down with such force that I was worried alcohol would spill onto her hand, her blue eyes full of surprise. "Indy, you haven't even exchanged phone numbers?" she asked incredulously, pushing her strawberry-blonde hair over her shoulder. "You've gone on two dates. How do you communicate? And how did I not know this?"

"Three dates," I corrected. "And we always message each other through the dating app. You know that I don't give out my number right away for safety reasons."

"Serial killer."

"What?" I was confused.

"You either think he's a serial killer or he thinks you're a serial killer. That's why you haven't swapped numbers."

"I am not a serial killer."

Leslie put a finger to her chest. "*I* know you're not a serial killer. But does Joel know that?"

"Of course."

She picked up a fry and pointed it at me. "But you didn't say he wasn't a killer. Maybe you secretly think he'll murder you in your sleep."

I shook my head. "You need to stop listening to so many true-crime podcasts."

"Never. But seriously, do you have any subconscious reservations about him?"

I dug deep and really thought about the question before answering, "Well…"

"Well what?" Leslie probed.

"I don't think he's a bad guy, but I do worry he might be too much of a good guy."

She smiled knowingly and pointed at me. "You think he's going to be a dud in bed."

"The thought has occurred to me."

"Personally, bad sex is still sex. And you, my friend, need to get laid. You've been crabby. How long has it been?"

"Too long."

"How long?"

I sighed. "About sixteen months."

"No wonder you're such a bitch."

I picked up a fry and threw it at her. "Just because you get some on the regular doesn't mean you can call me names."

Leslie laughed. "Okay, how about bitchy? My sweet, mild-mannered friend has been bitchy for the last few months."

I rolled my eyes. "You wouldn't be completely wrong. I have been on edge recently. But I don't agree about the bad-sex thing. Nothing's worse than having to sneak off to the bathroom to get yourself off after doing the deed because he got his and I didn't."

Leslie made a disgusted face. "Have I ever told you how much I dislike your ex?"

"Constantly," I said dryly.

"Good. I just wanted to make sure you knew to never get back together with him."

"He's already got a new girlfriend. You have nothing to worry about."

Leslie took a drink of her beer. "So, Mr. Bad Sex is getting some, and you're not. Criminal, Indy. That is criminal."

I shrugged. "So, what do I do?"

The server chose that moment to show up.

"You're young and good-looking," Leslie said to him.

"Uh...thanks."

"Don't worry. I'm not hitting on you. I need a man's perspective on this."

The guy relaxed. "Shoot."

"My friend here met this guy on a dating app. They've gone on three dates, but neither of them has gone home with the other. Don't you think that's weird? My friend needs to get laid. Do you think the guy is putting her off? What should she do?"

The server whistled while I covered my eyes.

"Thanks for laying it all out there like that, Leslie."

She held up her hands. "Hey, how is…" She paused to look at his name tag. "How is Graham here supposed to give us his full opinion if he doesn't know all the details?"

I dropped my hand and looked at Graham. "Sorry for putting you on the spot."

Graham shrugged. "It breaks up the monotony. And I'd rather have something like this happen at one of my tables than have someone yell at me because their order was wrong."

"I'm glad my love life—or lack thereof—is here to amuse you," I told him.

Leslie leaned closer to Graham. "Sorry about my friend. She's crabby because she hasn't gotten laid in quite a while."

I rolled my eyes.

"Hey, I'm just saying, what kind of guy doesn't want to get laid?"

Graham rubbed his jaw. "He might have his reasons. Maybe he really likes you and wants to take it slow."

Leslie snorted. "They haven't even exchanged phone numbers. I think it's weird they've only been messaging through the dating app."

Graham lifted his chin. "Where's your phone?"

I pulled my cell from my purse. "Here."

"Pull up the app and send him a message. Ask him for

4

his phone number. Tell him it's time you got more personal."

"I don't know," I said hesitantly.

Leslie snatched the phone from my hand and started tapping away.

I realized I could easily take it back but didn't bother. I was on my second glass of beer, so while I wasn't buzzed enough to drunk-text, I was loose enough to let my friend do it for me.

Graham moved behind Leslie and watched her type.

"How does that sound?" she asked him.

He nodded. "Good."

"And send," Leslie said and handed my phone back to me.

I quickly looked at what she'd written.

> Me: Hey. We've gone on three dates now, and I like you. What do you say we get off this dating app and you give me your phone number?

A second later, a message popped up.

> Joel: Why do you want my phone number?

I read the message out loud. I couldn't tell if he was flirting back or if he was being evasive.

Leslie snatched my phone back.

"What are you typing?" I asked.

She didn't answer. Instead, she typed away and handed it back.

Me: How else am I supposed to call you and whisper dirty things in your ear?

I looked up at my best friend. "Really? I can't believe you sent that."

She shrugged and took a sip of her drink. "If he doesn't give it to you after that, he doesn't like you, or he's a serial killer."

Graham moved back in between us. "Serial killer?"

"Yeah," Leslie said in a *duh* tone. "He doesn't want his number traced back to him after he kills Indy."

"Thanks," I said.

She shrugged. "If the shoe fits…"

Graham laughed. "You're weird. But this has been fun." He looked at me. "Good luck."

"Thanks."

Graham walked away, and my phone pinged.

Leslie rubbed her hands together. "Moment of truth."

Joel: 651-555-3825

"He gave me his number," I said in surprise. I hadn't realized how much I'd thought he'd say no until then.

"Maybe he's not a serial killer after all," Leslie said.

I looked up from my phone. "That sounds very reassuring."

She shrugged. "That's what I'm here for."

TWO

INDY

DESPITE LESLIE'S URGINGS, I did not go home after dinner and text Joel to come over. I didn't want to appear desperate, and I thought I secretly wanted to make him squirm.

But by Saturday night, when he hadn't messaged me on the dating app to ask why I hadn't texted him yet, I broke down and pulled up my phone.

I was comfortable enough with myself to admit that I liked alpha males and guys who went after what they wanted, and it was becoming apparent that Joel was more of a beta male. And while it made him less attractive in my eyes, the alpha male thing hadn't worked out for me so far. I needed to change things up and try something new.

That was why I was lying on my couch with my thumb hovering over the Send button.

"Just do it, Indy," I told myself out loud. "You have nothing to lose."

I closed my eyes and hit the button.

> Me: I need you to come over. I want to feel you inside me.

I reread my text and cringed. Leslie had told me that I needed to be forward and not hold back, but now, I wondered if my text was over the top.

I guessed I was going to find out.

> Joel: Who is this?

> Me: Indy.

After a moment, I started having doubts. I could be texting the wrong person.

> Me: Who's this? I'm looking for Gentleman7487.

I purposely used Joel's username, so he would know it was me.

> Joel: Wrong number.

Fuck my life. So, it wasn't Joel I was texting. I hated that I was right.

> Me: Oh crap. I'm sorry. I must have gotten the number wrong.

I opened the dating app and double-checked. It was the number he'd given me. I started typing a message to Joel to tell him he'd given me the wrong digits when a message popped up.

Not Joel: I'm not. What's your address?

I switched to my text messages, abandoning my message to Joel.

Me: I can't tell you that. We don't even know each other.

Not Joel: I know enough to know that you need to be fucked well and good.

I swallowed and grew wet between my legs.
Damn my attraction to dirty-talkers.

Me: That might be true. But how do I know that you won't murder me after?

Not Joel: I guess you don't. But I can promise you I've never murdered anyone. The extent of my killing has gone no further than spiders.

Me: I respect that. I hate spiders.

Not Joel: So, what do you say? Am I coming over or not?

Me: How do we know we'll be attracted to each other?

Not Joel: We don't. I guess we'll find out when we meet.

Me: Just so you know, if I say yes, I'm screenshotting everything and sending it to my best friend in case I go missing.

Not Joel: Good idea. Women can never be too safe. But just so you know, the only thing you'll be missing after I'm done with you is your ability to walk.

Me: I need you to answer four questions before I say yes.

I swallowed. I couldn't believe I was actually considering this.

Not Joel: Hit me.

Me: 1. Are you between the ages of 25 and 40?

I wasn't having sex with someone who was illegal, so I wanted a safe distance from anyone under eighteen. Also, at thirty-one, I didn't want anyone more than ten years younger than me. And my parents were in their early fifties. I wasn't going to have sex with anyone closer to their age than mine.

Me: 2. What kind of car do you drive?

This was another safety measure. And maybe it would give me more insight to the stranger I was seriously thinking of inviting over for sex.

Me: 3. What is your name?

That was an obvious question. I wanted to stop calling him Not Joel in my head.

> Me: 4. Can you send a pic of yourself?

This was the big one. If he sent me a dick pic, I was out. Also, if he sent me a toothless grin, I was out. *#imshallowandiknowit.* This was someone I'd potentially sleep with. I felt I was allowed a little shallowness. Lastly, I wanted something to confirm his age.

I hit Send and waited to see what he'd say or if he'd blow me off.

> **Not Joel:**
> 1. Yes, I'm 38.
>
> 2. I drive a three-year-old BMW X3.
>
> 3. You can call me Cal. And you are again?

I read the first three, feeling pretty satisfied. He wasn't too old and thankfully not too young. I preferred older men anyway. He drove a BMW, which could mean he was a pompous ass, but the fact that it was an SUV rather than a sports car and three years old made me feel like he might be more down-to-earth. The name Cal was kind of sexy. I figured it was short for Calvin, which was less sexy, but I wasn't going to ask.

And that was when I knew I was going to go through with this as long as question four was answered in the way I wanted. I didn't want him to confirm his name was in fact Calvin and then have it turn me off. I already had it bad for this guy. Not every man could come up with some dirty texts that stayed on the right side of sexy versus corny.

I bit my lip and mentally crossed my fingers that he wouldn't send me a dick pic, and when the picture came through, I was rewarded. Very handsomely.

He was lying on a couch, and I could see a television on in the background. The show playing on the screen was less than five years old, so I knew he hadn't sent me something from twenty years ago. This guy was just racking up the points.

The picture had been taken in low light, but there was enough of a glow to see he wore jeans and had a very impressive six-pack. I could also see the bottom of his face. He looked to be his age with dark stubble and a sexy-as-sin mouth.

I immediately pictured it kissing me all over my body.

I sank down in my couch and squeezed my thighs together. I wanted to touch myself, but I refused because what I wanted more was to wait for him—for Cal.

But before I texted him back, I had to check one thing first.

I downloaded the image he'd sent and did a reverse image search on the internet. I'd been tricked by a stock photo or two in the past, so it was now the first thing I checked.

The internet pulled up similar photos but nothing matching the one he'd sent me, and I practically giggled with excitement. And then I laughed out loud at myself for acting like a grade-schooler with her first crush.

> Me: I'm Indy. And here's a little something from me.

I pulled off my shirt and pumped up my medium-sized breasts in my unfortunately plain bra. I showed about as much face as he had—that way, if it ended up on the internet, I wasn't naked, and no one would be able to tell who I was anyway.

> Cal: This is the part where you tell me no and this has all been a joke, right? Because there is no way someone as sexy as you doesn't have someone to fuck you properly.

God. The man was hot.

> Cal: Either way, thanks for the entertainment tonight. I haven't had this much fun in a long time.

My only reply was to send him my address.

THREE
CAL

I STARED down at my phone as Indy's address came through along with another text.

Indy: Bring condoms.

"Hey, asshole. It's your turn. Quit staring at your phone," my younger cousin Travis said.

I looked up at my friends sitting around the poker table. If I walked away now, I'd be leaving a lot of money. But at the same time, I hadn't had this much excitement in forever.

And I hadn't been laid in months.

The thought of getting my dick wet had the fucker standing at full attention under the table.

I set my cards down. "I fold."

The group erupted in groans and protests.

"Come on, man. You can't leave now. You're one of our best players," Caleb, Travis's brother-in-law, said.

"Sorry," I said and stood. "But I'll see you guys again next week."

As I headed for the entrance, Travis called out, "If we even invite you."

I laughed and closed the door behind me.

Since I'd moved back to the Minneapolis–St. Paul area from New York, my family and old friends had welcomed me home, including inviting me to their occasional poker games. And while I appreciated it, I was itching for something different.

The irony was, I had moved back home because I had gotten sick of the busy pace of Manhattan, but I'd told everyone it was because I wanted to be closer to family. It was partially true. My parents were getting older. Both my brother and sister had kids, and I didn't want to miss out on that. But my main motivator had been that I needed to slow down.

When your doctor told you that there was a good chance your stressful job could have you dead by forty if you didn't make some changes in your life, you listened.

But now, here I was, getting bored with life, which was why I liked the distraction of receiving a text from Indy.

I'd been so busy with work the last few years that I hadn't even taken the time to dirty-text with someone. Seeing her text about how she wanted to feel me inside her had woken something in me.

Even if she hadn't meant the text for me, my cock didn't care. And quite frankly, neither did I.

I stopped at a gas station on my way to her address and picked up condoms. I made sure to get a full box of Magnums. I was probably being selfish, inviting myself over, but I was going to make sure we both ended up satisfied.

When I pulled up to Indy's modest house, I parked on

the curb. She only lived about twenty minutes from me in a suburb that looked nice and quiet. I didn't want to give the neighbors anything to talk about by parking in the driveway.

I walked up to the door and knocked. A cute brunette with brown eyes answered. She was average height with an average build. She was very girl-next-door, except when it came to her mouth. It was sexy as fuck. And the glimpse I had gotten in the picture she sent me was nothing compared to real life.

I hadn't really been concerned too much how beautiful or not beautiful she was because men who judged women by their looks were pricks.

But attraction? That was different. The attraction, the chemistry, was needed, or neither of us was going to enjoy ourselves in the bedroom.

And I could practically feel the sparks coming off the two of us.

I was going to fuck her so good.

Indy held out her hand. "I'm Indy. Nice to meet you."

I took her hand and pushed her back, so we both were in the house now. I kicked the door closed behind me and maneuvered her until her back hit the wall.

"Cal," I said, introducing myself. I moved our connected hands up over her head, and I leaned in close. The heat in her eyes flared, and I knew the answer before I even asked, "Are we doing this?"

"Oh, yes," she said.

I smirked and took her lips, holding nothing back.

She immediately opened up, and I licked inside her mouth. One of her legs wrapped around the back of mine, and I knew this was going to be an epic fucking experience.

I picked her up by her ass and lifted her into my arms. My bag of condoms hit my leg, reminding me that we needed to get to a nice, big bed where I could take my time.

"Bedroom?" I asked.

She pointed behind me, and I followed her finger. "Down the hall, to the right."

I quickly carried her as she sucked on my neck and tried to move her pussy against my hardness.

It felt like the longest hallway even though it was a small house with only three doors. Most likely, two bedrooms and a bathroom, but it might as well have been fifty rooms.

Her bedroom door was slightly closed, and I banged it open as I entered. "Sorry," I said even though I really didn't care one way or another. I wasn't rich, but I would pay for any damage if that meant I got her naked that much sooner.

Indy laughed. "Someone's in a hurry."

I threw the condoms on the nightstand and her on the bed. "Hell yes, I am. I need to get inside you before you realize you're about to fuck a stranger and change your mind."

She moaned. "If you keep talking like that, I will do whatever you want. Plus, this isn't my first one-night stand, although I do admit it's been a while since I had one."

"Same here," I said as I stripped off my shirt.

She sat up and ran her hands over my abdomen. "Oh God, they're even better in real life."

The picture I had sent her had been taken by an ex who dabbled as a photographer. It had been taken a few years ago, and while I was now on the older side, it was nice to know I didn't disappoint.

I smiled at her compliment and reached for her shirt. I

pulled it over her head and pushed her back against the bed. I drew one cup of her bra down and sucked a nipple in my mouth.

She whimpered and arched her hips.

"These look better in real life too," I said, reaching behind her and unclipping her bra. I tugged it off and threw it across the room. "Even better," I said.

I moved to the other breast and teased her nipple with my tongue and teeth.

Indy reached between us and cupped my erection. "I really like that you weren't a sleaze by sending me a dick pic, but damn, I might have made an exception if I had known you were packing this much heat."

I drew her hands up over her head and went for her pants. "A gentleman never brags. And dick pics are exactly what you said. Sleazy. Unless a woman asks for it. That's the only exception." I dragged her pants down and off.

She smiled. "And has a woman ever asked for one?"

I grinned. "A gentleman also never tells."

I gently pushed two fingers inside her and hissed. "Fuck. You are so wet. And tight."

She rocked her hips on my hand. "It's been a while."

I shook my head and unbuttoned my jeans. "Whoever that guy you meant to text is, he's a fucking idiot."

"How do you know that?"

"Because I'm here and he's not."

I took my pants off with one hand as I rubbed her G-spot with my other. When I withdrew my hands to use them to grab a condom and put it on, she whimpered.

Once I was ready to go, I climbed over her and kissed her again. As she threaded her fingers in my hair, I nudged her entrance with my cock. I took my time, going slow as I guided my length inside her.

Despite her tightness, she opened for me, and the grip of her pussy was absolutely perfect.

I rocked in and out at first, letting her get used to the feel of me. But when her nails scored the skin of my back, I couldn't wait any longer. I drove inside her, not holding back my power, but I was rewarded with her sweet cries as she came apart within minutes.

Her pussy squeezed me hard, and my cock started to jump. At that point, I knew it was over for me, too, and I exploded inside her.

FOUR
INDY

MONDAY MORNING, I walked off the elevator, only to be ambushed by Leslie.

"Girl, where have you been?"

I looked at my watch. "I'm ten minutes early."

She grabbed my hand and pulled me into the restroom. She checked under each stall and then turned to me and crossed her arms. "The last thing I heard from you was your screenshots of your conversation with a sexy stranger. I thought I was your best friend."

I frowned. "I texted you last night, telling you I was okay and still alive. I even used our code word, so you'd for sure know it was me."

She threw her hands up. "Yeah, and you didn't give me *any* details. How dare you."

I laughed. "I wasn't ready. I was half in a sex coma."

After our first round of sex, I'd thrown a hand on his chest and told him I needed another round before he left. The sex had been that good. He'd ended up staying all night and half the next day. It was the best one-nighter I'd ever had.

Leslie fell back against the sink, a hand on her chest. "I'm so jealous."

"You have sex on the regular."

She stood straight. "Not with some guy I don't know. The mystery, the unknown, the secrecy. So fucking hot."

I tilted my head. "Aren't those three items just different words for the same thing?"

She shrugged. "Maybe, but that's how hot it is. Like I said, I'm jealous."

"You could always text some stranger and see what happens."

Her shoulder sagged. "With my luck, I'd get someone's eighty-year-old grandma, and I'd give her a heart attack with my sex talk."

"You're dark."

She lifted a shoulder. "Besides, I kind of agreed with Asher that we wouldn't sleep with anyone else."

I fake gasped. "What? Leslie Hale is going monogamous?"

"Fuck you," she said and headed for the door.

I chased after her. "Tell me more."

"No."

I laughed, and she smiled at me.

"I'll tell you all about it later."

We rounded the corner, away from the restroom area and toward our cubicles, when Angela, a coworker, stopped us.

"Are you guys ready?"

Leslie and I exchanged looks.

"Ready for what?" I asked.

"The new boss starts today," Angela said, her eyes wide.

Leslie and I both groaned.

Our old boss was the best person I'd ever worked for. She was assertive yet approachable. And as a woman, she totally understood what it was like to be a female in the workplace. She had really improved the company, making it a popular name in this part of the Midwest. Which was probably why someone from Silicon Valley had snatched her up. We'd all been sad to see her go.

Except for maybe my and Leslie's immediate supervisor. Patrick hadn't liked working for a woman. He never said it, but we all knew it. It wasn't any wonder why the women on our team barely got along with him. I wished someone from Silicon Valley would hire him and take him away, but the chances of that happening were slim. The only one who thought he was the best in the business was himself.

"I want Polly back," I said with a pout.

"Me too," Leslie agreed.

"We have a video conference with the Chicago office in five minutes, where they're going to introduce Nicholas Callan," Angela said.

"Who the hell is Nicholas Callan?" Leslie said.

"The new boss," Angela said in a tone that suggested she couldn't believe Leslie didn't know his name.

Leslie looked at me, and I shook my head. I hadn't known his name either. Truthfully, I'd been ignoring all news of a new boss like a petulant child whose favorite toy had been taken away. My favorite toy being Polly, our old boss.

I knew I would eventually have to make nice with the new boss, but I wasn't going to do it until the last minute.

Wanting to get away from Angela's intensity, I said, "We'd better go and get ready then."

Angela nodded. "Right. Good idea."

She walked away, and Leslie rolled her eyes. "She makes a big deal out of everything."

I laughed. "She can be a little much, but she has a good heart."

The two of us headed toward our cubicles. Polly had been so cool that she let the both of us sit by each other even though she knew we were close friends. We might only have seven people on our whole team, plus our supervisor, so we'd never be far away from one another, but Polly could have put us on opposite ends if she wanted to.

Leslie nudged me. "Good thing you got laid this weekend, or you'd have been extra crabby about the new boss."

I held up a finger to protest.

"Don't even try to deny it," Leslie said.

"Okay, you *might* be right. That's all you're getting from me."

Leslie laughed and pulled out her chair when we reached our spots.

I put my purse in my drawer, took my seat, and turned on my laptop. I looked at Leslie. "If the new boss fires me, do you promise to quit in solidarity?" I asked.

"You're not going to get fired."

"Okay, if I get laid off, do you promise?"

She snarled. "If this guy comes in and starts making changes for the 'sake of the company,' " she said, using air quotes, "I will follow you out the door so fast that they won't be able to tell where you end and I begin."

"Aw…that's the sweetest thing you've ever said to me," I

joked. "Seriously though, I'm with you. I refuse to work for someone who cuts staff before even getting to know how things work or what people do around here."

Leslie held up her pinkie finger, and I shook it with my own. The two of us had been together since college, and no one was breaking us up now.

The big projector screen lit up, and we knew it was time to meet the new boss.

We were a software company that had originated out of Chicago, so we often did video conferences with the office there. We only had about seventy-five employees in a large, open floor plan so that everyone could see the screen. Only a few rooms had doors that closed—the boss's office, a conference room for meetings, and a couple of private rooms for when people needed a quiet atmosphere to think.

The company liked making everyone feel like they were all on the same level and teammates rather than coworkers, but sometimes, some of us needed to be alone and to get away from the noise of the other employees.

Leslie and my team were toward the back of the room, so when the CEO of the company, Mr. Malone, and the president, Mr. Randu, came on and began talking about Polly's departure and Nicholas Callan's entrance, I pulled up my work email and began to do some cleaning. I was going to play nice with the new boss, but I couldn't care less to hear about him and his background.

Blah, blah, blah.

Leslie kicked me, and I looked up.

"And with that, I'd like to introduce you to Nicholas Callan," the CEO said, and the door to Polly's old office opened.

I waited for the new boss to step out and make his dramatic entrance. I already knew I wasn't going to like him.

Keith—who had been Polly's old assistant and was now Nicholas Callan's new assistant—blocked our view from the back. I caught a glimpse of dark hair and a nice suit as the two of them walked to the front, and I stifled a groan. Our workplace was business casual. Basically, the rule was no jeans and no shorts, except on Fridays. If this guy was in a suit, he was probably going to be an arrogant prick.

That's right; I was judging the guy before I even knew him. Sue me.

But when Keith stepped away, I choked on a gasp.

"What's wrong?" Leslie said.

I gripped the arms of the chair, too frozen to answer her.

I now knew what Cal stood for.

It was short for Callan. And it was way sexier than Calvin.

I'd just spent the last day and a half fucking the new boss. I was so screwed.

This time, not in a good way.

FIVE
INDY

I HID behind my computer as best I could. I really doubted Cal—*Nicholas Callan* would notice me, but I wasn't taking chances.

"Hello, everyone," he greeted us with a confident smile and head nod. "Thank you for the welcome." He looked over his shoulder at the screen. "And thank you to our wonderful CEO and president for the introduction."

"Yawn," Leslie said beside me, patting her open mouth.

I snort-laughed despite my inner panic.

"I trust you have it from here," the CEO said before he and the president made their goodbyes and clicked off.

"Now that he's gone," our new boss said, "let me tell you a few things about me."

Leslie leaned over to me, and I wanted to kick her. She was going to get us caught for not paying attention, and then he would see me.

"I might be bored, but he is super fine."

I just nodded, so she'd go back to her own area.

But she was right. He had dark, almost black hair, and green eyes. They sparkled when he had sex.

I dropped my head in my hands. That was something an employee was *not* supposed to know about their new boss. But I didn't know how I was going to forget it.

Right now, all I could picture was how determined he'd been to make me come when he was inside me. I'd never been with someone so focused on pleasuring me.

My core flooded with heat, and I whimpered softly.

"What's wrong?" Leslie asked.

I shook my head. "Nothing."

I'd tell her later. After Cal was safely in his office. Or maybe after we were safely out of the building.

I forced my eyes open because closing them had only brought back memories, and I stared blankly at my computer.

I heard a pair of hands clap, and I looked up at the boss. It had been him.

Oh God, did he notice I wasn't paying attention?

I watched him, but he didn't look my way, so I relaxed.

"I know having a new boss is not easy, and I want to alleviate everyone's fears about big changes coming. I know this place runs well, and I don't plan on doing anything to ruin that."

"Damn right it does," Leslie said.

"Thanks, everyone, and we'll be talking soon."

Nicholas Callan headed back to his office, and I breathed a sigh of relief.

"That wasn't so bad," Leslie said. "He seems like a nice guy."

In bed? Yes. In the office? We'll have to see.

"Indy?"

I turned to my best friend.

"You were zoned out. Are you sure you're okay?"

I opened my mouth to tell her that our new manager was Cal, Mr. Wrong Number, when Patrick walked over.

"Leslie, Indy, where are you on the Glessan software?"

"I think we'll be done by the end of the week," I answered for the both of us.

"Make it Wednesday. The client is waiting for us."

The contract actually stated we'd have it to them by the end of the month, which was over three weeks away. We had plenty of time to get our part of the project submitted. Patrick just wanted to throw his weight around, but both of us were past letting him get to us.

"You wouldn't want us to compromise quality, now would you?" Leslie asked.

Polly had never put up with his shit, and if the new boss sided with him and Patrick fired me, then it would just save me from embarrassment of facing Cal.

He was trying to intimidate the wrong women.

"We'll have it by Friday, just like we promised from the beginning." I smiled sweetly. "Okay?"

Patrick murmured something, looked at the guy sitting next to Leslie, who had heard the whole thing, and told him to get to work, and then he walked off.

I gave him the finger. It was behind my cubicle wall because while I might stand up for myself, I wasn't dumb enough to get caught flipping off my supervisor.

"What were you going to say?" Leslie asked.

"Huh?"

"You were about to say something before Patrick came over."

"Oh. I don't remember." I remembered, but after that interruption, I figured it wasn't a good idea to tell her anything when anyone could eavesdrop.

I went to work to the point that I actually put Nicholas Callan out of my mind, but then Keith had to come around and ruin everything.

"Hey, ladies. After lunch, Mr. Callan is going to start meeting with everyone in the office."

My belly flipped. "What?" I demanded.

Keith grinned. "Yeah, it's great. He wants to get to know everyone here and talk with them. He actually wants to hear what we have to say."

"That sounds awesome," Leslie said.

"Doesn't it though?" Keith agreed. He pulled his tablet back from his chest and looked at it. "So, Leslie, I have you down for around two-ish. It just depends on how long everyone takes. He said he doesn't want to rush anything, so it might be before or later. I'll let you know."

"Got it," Leslie said.

"And, Indy..." Keith scanned the page. "Where are you? Where are you?" He rolled his eyes and laughed. "I didn't see you because you're way at the top." He looked at me and smiled. "Second person of the day. You're lucky."

"Put in a good word for me," Leslie joked to me.

"I'll try," I said, but there was no way I was meeting with him.

I needed to figure out what I was going to do.

SIX

INDY

THE THOUGHT of faking my own death crossed my mind, but instead, I told Leslie I was going to run out and grab some lunch. Then, I just never went back. I sent her a text to tell Patrick I was sick.

I needed a new game plan, but I didn't want to think about it, and rather than facing my problem head-on, I decided to ignore it for the rest of the night.

That's right; I decided to hide from the world.

I turned off my phone, picked up food from the drive-through, and went home and watched Netflix the rest of the night. I was going to drown myself in someone else's fake problems while I avoided my own.

It seemed like a solid plan until I woke up an hour earlier than normal the next morning. Turned out that not looking at your phone all night helped you get to bed at a decent time. Who knew?

I showered, and then I headed for the office while I listened to my voice mails and tried to come up with a new game plan. Maybe I could convince Keith to take me off the list.

"Indy, this is your mom. Where are you? Leslie called me and said she couldn't get ahold of you. Please let me know you're okay. I love you. Bye."

Next message.

"Indy, you are on my shit list. I have texted you a dozen times and called you a dozen more. I even called your mom to see if she knew what had happened to you."

I snorted. "Yeah, I know you called my mom."

"You did not seem sick at work, and then you just disappeared. You're lucky I'm busy tonight, or I'd come over to your house and break your door down. Now, please call me."

I also had what felt like a million texts, but I couldn't read them until I got to work. Not that it was much of a mystery who had messaged me. Leslie was very tenacious when she wanted something.

I pulled into work, excited to be the first one there. I said hi to the security guard, who thankfully wasn't one who liked to chat, and headed to my floor. Once I got there, I grabbed my computer and other things I needed and made a beeline for one of the private rooms.

They couldn't make me talk to the new boss if they couldn't find me.

I turned on my computer and sent Leslie a text.

> Me: I'm alive and at work. You can find me in private room 2.

I waited a few minutes to see if she would answer before

I started playing catch-up for the stuff I'd missed yesterday from leaving early.

She didn't answer, and I got to work.

About an hour later, I could hear the sounds of my coworkers arriving and knew it wouldn't be long before Leslie found me hiding out.

The door burst open, and it felt like a whirlwind had arrived when my friend made her entrance.

"All right, young lady, spill it."

I arched my neck, trying to see if anyone had heard her.

"No one's out there."

I sank down in my seat. "Close the door, will you?"

She shut the door and sat down across from me. "What is going on?"

I took a deep breath. "I don't want to meet the new boss."

She frowned in confusion. "Why? I heard he's actually a really nice guy. I haven't had my chance to talk to him yet, but I think he might not be as bad as we thought he was going to be."

I shook my head. "It's not that."

"Then, what is it?"

Even though we were alone, I leaned forward and whispered, "The new boss, Nicholas *Cal*lan is Cal."

It took a few seconds for Leslie to catch on to my words, but when she did, she burst out laughing.

"*Shh*, I don't want anyone to know I'm in here."

Leslie tried to be quiet, but she couldn't stop laughing.

"That is the fucking best thing I have heard all year. You fucked the boss. You are so screwed."

"Thank you. Thank you very much," I said dryly.

That only made her laugh harder.

"You're a bitch, and I hate you."

Leslie wiped the tears from the corners of her eyes. "I'm sorry, Indy, but I can't help it. That is seriously the funniest thing I've heard. I'm going to remember it forever."

I scowled at her, and she suddenly sat up in her seat and gasped.

"Give me your phone."

"Why?" I asked suspiciously.

"I want to see that pic he sent you. All I have is a screenshot of it in your message."

"I deleted it," I lied.

"Yeah, right." She didn't believe me, but she let it go. "Listen, you can't tell anyone. I don't know what I'm going to do."

"You could quit."

I looked at her.

"I'm kidding. Of course, you can't quit. I refuse to be here without you."

"And that's why I'm hiding. I know, sooner or later, he's going to find out, but the longer I put it off, the better."

There was a knock at the door, and Keith popped his head in. "There you are, Indy. Since you went home sick yesterday, I have you first on the list to meet with Mr. Callan this morning."

I looked at Leslie with *help me* eyes.

She shrugged. "Sorry, babe. It looks like it's going to be sooner rather than later."

I dragged my heels as I walked toward the office, and I tried to come up with any excuse as to why I couldn't go in.

I came up with squat.

The office was made up of all windows, so we could normally see inside. But the floor-to-ceiling blinds were closed today. I couldn't even get a good look at him before walking inside.

Keith raised his eyebrows. "You can go in. He's waiting for you."

"Thanks. No pressure or anything."

He rolled his eyes. "Don't be dramatic. You'll be fine," he said and turned to open the door.

I took a deep breath, flapped my arms to relieve the sweat that had started to gather in my pits, and put on a straight face.

You can do this, Indy. He's just a guy.

I walked in behind Keith and saw Cal—Mr. Callan…I didn't know what to call him anymore—standing off to the side, looking at some papers. He still didn't look like the guy who'd come to my house in jeans and a black T-shirt, but at least he'd lost the suit. He had on a button-down shirt with the sleeves rolled up, which showed off his muscular fore-arms, and dark navy pants that fit his ass like they had been tailored for him. They probably had been, but that thought didn't stop me from having to almost wipe the drool from my mouth.

I thought he'd gotten hotter since our night together.

That brought back memories, and I smiled to myself. I wondered if the reason he was standing was because he couldn't sit since I'd left claw marks on his cheeks. I doubted it, but it was a fun thought that helped relieve some nerves.

"Mr. Callan, this is Indy Scott," Keith said, and I lost my smile.

Nicholas Callan looked up from whatever he had been reading and gave me a polite smile. Too polite. There was no recognition in his eyes.

"Hello," he said as he walked to his desk. He gestured out his hand. "Have a seat, please."

I took the chair in front of his desk as he sat behind his without a single wince. It appeared his butt was fine, and I was a little disappointed. I'd been suffering the last twenty-four hours. He should have been suffering a little too.

"Keith told me you were sick yesterday?"

Not in the traditional sense, but I had felt nauseated. "Yes."

He studied me but not in a sexy way. In the way a boss studied their employees. "But you're feeling better today?"

My stomach was in knots, and I had the cold sweats. "Not one hundred percent, but better."

"That's good." He sat back in his seat and picked up a folder. "It says you've worked here for five years?"

"Almost six," I said.

He put the folder down and met my eyes. Still nothing in his gaze to let me know that he knew who I was. His green eyes were serious.

"And do you like it here?"

Is he trying to get rid of me?

"I love it." *Take that. You're not kicking me out of here without a fight.*

He smiled. "That's good. Exactly what a new boss wants to hear when starting in a company."

I smiled back, but I wasn't sure if it reached my eyes.

Is this guy for real?

He'd literally been inside me two days ago, and today, he was making small talk like we'd never met.

And now, I was thinking of him inside me.

Don't turn red, don't turn red, don't turn red. And for God's sake, don't squirm.

It was the hardest thing I'd ever done, but I was pretty confident that I hadn't moved a single muscle. I felt some heat hit my cheeks, but I'd said that I didn't feel back to normal, and thankfully, he was looking down at the folder again.

"It also says here that your real name is Lucinda?"

He looked up, and I gave him a second to acknowledge my arousal. He did no such thing.

"It was my grandmother's name, and she went by Lucy, so they called me Indy." I tilted my head to the side, deciding it was time to test him. "Do you have any nicknames, Mr. Callan?"

"Oh, a few," he said with a straight face. No cocky smirk, no glint in his eye, not even a slight smile.

I was beginning to think I'd dreamed the whole sex encounter. I must have seen his pictures somewhere in the office, and I was now going insane.

"What would you like us to call you? We called our last boss by her first name. Do you go by Nicholas? Nick?"

"God, no. Nicholas is my father's name. You can call me Cal."

You can call me Cal.

Those were the same words he'd texted me the night he came over. So, maybe I wasn't crazy.

A throat cleared behind me, and I jumped. I'd forgotten Keith was still in the room.

Cal looked up at his assistant. "Some people refuse to call me by my preferred name."

"It's not personal," I said. "Keith called Polly, our last boss, Ms. Dyer until the day she left. You're never going to get him to change."

Keith sniffed. "It's the professional thing to do."

I rolled my eyes, and Cal grinned at me. It wasn't a knowing grin or a secret grin, but it was the first sign that this was the same guy who had come over to my house the other night.

"Listen, it was great talking to you," Cal said. "If you ever need anything, my door is open."

Again, his face was straight, and there was no sexual innuendo in his voice.

He stood and held out his hand. "It was nice meeting you."

"You too," I said and placed my hand in his to shake.

Electricity shot up my arm, just like it had on Saturday when he came to my house.

I needed to go and get some fresh air.

I dropped his hand. "Thanks," I muttered and hurried for the door.

SEVEN

INDY

LESLIE POPPED out of nowhere a few feet away from the office, and I cried out, clasping a hand to my chest.

"You scared me."

She ignored me. "Oh my God, what did he say? Did he flirt with you? Did he take you over his desk?"

I gave her a *really* look. "Keith was there the whole time."

"Whoa. You had sex in front of Keith? Mr. Boss Man is a bad boy."

"Nothing happened," I hissed. "I mean, nothing. He acted like he was meeting me for the first time."

Leslie wrinkled her nose. "Well, there goes my entertainment for the day."

"Thanks a lot."

"Hey, I don't want you to suffer any more than you are, but since you are, I might as well enjoy myself."

"You're the worst best friend ever."

"I took all your stuff from the private room back to your desk," she said in a singsong voice.

"Thank you. I suppose you've moved from the top ten list to the top one hundred." I stepped around her and headed for my cubicle.

Leslie was right behind me. "So, he really didn't say anything about the weekend?"

"Not a word."

"Bummer." She dropped down in her chair and shrugged. "But it looks like you were worried for nothing."

I sat down. "Yeah, maybe. I guess we'll see."

My phone buzzed under the pile of my stuff that Leslie had carried over.

> Cal: What were you thinking about when you turned red in my office? You couldn't seem to sit still.

I whipped my head up, but the blinds were still closed.

Then, at that moment, Keith opened them. Cal was at his desk but not looking in my direction.

Leslie sat forward in her chair. "What?"

"Act normal," I told her.

"What?"

"Act. Normal. Get on your computer or something."

"Not until you tell me what happened."

"I will once you get on your computer," I said, teeth clenched.

"You two bicker like an old married couple," Tessa, a coworker, said as she walked past.

Leslie and I looked at each other and shrugged.

She pulled up her latest project on her laptop, her back to me. "Okay, will you tell me now?"

"Don't turn around, but he just texted me."

"Holy shit. What does it say?"

"I'll tell you everything later," I promised. "But all he has to do is look out his office window to see us talking. I don't want him to know I told you."

Leslie was quiet a minute. "Okay. I get it. I don't like it, but I get it." She looked over. "And I want to read every word later."

"Duh," I said.

She smiled and turned back around. "I can't wait," I heard her say.

I picked up my phone and bit my lip. I didn't know how to respond. He could be flirting with me, or he could just be acting like a boss as he had when we'd talked.

There was only one way to find out.

> Me: I was thinking about you being inside me.

I looked up at him, only to find him on his office phone. *Ugh.*

He probably wasn't going to read it for a long time. So much for my experiment.

Buzz.

> Cal: Fuck, Indy. You can't write stuff like that to me.

> Me: Because you're my boss now?

> Cal: No. Because I can't do anything about it. You don't know how badly I wanted to lay you down on my desk and take you right there.

Me: You sure didn't act like it.

Cal: Of course I didn't. I'm your boss. My new assistant would have called the Chicago office in a second.

Me: I don't know about that. Keith is pretty loyal to his bosses.

Cal: I don't think he'd be loyal if he knew the things I wanted to do to you.

Me: Like what?

Cal: I can't talk about that right now. I was already hard the whole time you were in here. I need to concentrate.

Me: Whatever you say. You're the boss.

I waited for him to respond again, but nothing came through.

Suppressing my disappointment, I set my phone down and got to work.

CAL

Not responding to Indy was tough, but I couldn't risk not paying attention to the immediate conversation.

I was on the phone with one of our biggest investors,

and he needed me to reassure him that nothing was going to change with the incoming new management.

But it was really hard to concentrate.

Seeing Indy walk through my office door had been like a punch in the gut. Or more like a punch in the dick.

When I'd left her house Sunday morning, I hadn't thought I'd ever see her again. Unless maybe either one of us needed some no-strings sex, which I wasn't exactly counting on.

It was a good thing I'd had some warning before she walked in, but I still hadn't been fully prepared.

When my assistant had told me that one of my staff that I was supposed to meet with had gone home sick, he'd given me her name and info. Indy wasn't a common name, and two minutes on the internet confirmed that one of my new employees was the woman I'd had sex with the weekend before.

I told Keith that I wanted to see Indy right away that morning. I suspected she hadn't really been sick and had left early when I made my introduction the day before. I needed to talk to her and let her know that I was aware of her existence. I wanted her to know that I considered her a part of the team and no different from any other employee.

That was the plan anyway.

But when she walked in, I wasn't ready for the instant attraction to hit me again. Or the memory of our night together. It didn't help that she looked sexy as hell.

She was dressed like any other coworker in the office, but I knew what she looked like underneath those clothes.

I was still determined to keep a professional distance—

until she turned red and squirmed in her seat. She looked turned on, guilty, and embarrassed, all at once.

I'd just had to know what she was thinking.

I picked up my cell as I pushed my office phone between my head and my shoulder. "Yes. Yes, sir, that's right," I said as I unlocked my phone and looked at her message again.

Indy: I was thinking about you being inside me.

I groaned as the blood rushed back to my groin. My dick had just started to go down after I read the message the first time.

"Mr. Callan, are you listening to me?" the investor demanded, sounding like a pompous asshole.

I had already confirmed what he wanted to know. Twice. I wasn't going to go through this again.

"I'm sorry, sir, but something just came to my attention. I'd best take care of it. We wouldn't want your hard-earned investment going to waste."

"No, we wouldn't," he reluctantly agreed.

"Have your assistant call mine, and we can set up another appointment." I ended the call and hung up the phone. "Keith?" I called from my open door.

Keith popped his head in the door. "Yes, Mr. Callan?"

Even though Indy had told me not to bother, I corrected him, "It's Cal. And when Mr. Bernard's assistant calls to set up an appointment, please don't schedule it for this week."

Keith smiled. "Sure thing, Mr. Callan."

"You can send in the next person for me to talk to."

"I'll be right back with Leslie Hale."

I pulled up her file while Keith went to get her. She was in the same division as Indy, and when I looked up to watch where Keith had gone, it looked like the two women sat next to each other.

They exchanged a few bits of conversation before Leslie came back to my office.

"Mr. Callan, Leslie Hale is here," Keith introduced her.

I stood. "Welcome, Leslie."

She marched up to me with a smile and held out her hand.

I shook it, and she looked disappointed.

"Damn," she said after she let go.

I raised my eyebrow, more wondering what she'd expected than her use of a curse word in the office, but I was a little impressed with her boldness.

"Pardon?" I asked.

She leaned forward and whispered, "I wanted to see if I felt a spark."

Leslie was tall and pretty with long strawberry-blonde hair and blue eyes, but she was right. There was no electricity between us.

Behind Leslie, I noticed Keith perk up where he stood against the wall. My guess was that he was trying to listen to what Leslie had to say.

I lowered my voice to match. "I take it, she told you."

I didn't need to be specific. She knew what I was talking about.

"Yes. She's my best friend."

I frowned. "Are we going to have a problem?"

Leslie lost her smile and looked startled, which was

good. I might be a nice guy, but I didn't take shit from my employees.

"No, sir, not at all. I was just having a little fun."

I raised my voice to normal. "In that case, you can call me Cal."

EIGHT

INDY

BY THE TIME I'd left work, Cal hadn't answered my question. He had only sent me one text, asking if Leslie was going to be a problem.

I'd basically looked at her and asked, "What did you do?"

She had shrugged and said it was no big deal and that she and Cal were on the same page. I hadn't quite believed her and made her promise not to do anything crazy.

When I got home that night, it finally occurred to me that I hadn't messaged Joel about how he'd sent me the wrong number. I'd been so consumed with Cal that I'd completely forgotten about the guy I'd gone out on three dates with.

I also thought it was weird that he hadn't asked why I hadn't texted him. It was Tuesday. I had asked him for his phone number on Friday. I had a strong feeling that he'd given me the wrong number on purpose.

I pulled up the dating app and sent Joel a message.

Me: Hey. So, I sent a text to the number you gave me, and the person told me I had the wrong number.

Joel: What? I'm sorry. I don't know how that happened. I think I had too much to drink at dinner. Maybe it's better if we just message each other on here.

That was a crock of shit.

Me: Yeah, I don't think so. I think you meant to give me the wrong number.

Joel: No, I didn't.

Me: Then, why didn't you message me all weekend, asking why I hadn't called or texted you?

Me: Don't worry. You don't have to answer that. It's because you knew you had given me a number that wasn't yours, so you weren't expecting anything.

Joel: That's not true.

Me: Okay. Prove it. Give me your number. Right now.

Joel: I can't.

This guy. I knew something was wrong.

Joel: It's my work phone. I can get in trouble.

Me: Bullshit.

Me: Goodbye, Joel. If that's even your name.

I didn't wait for him to answer. I just went to his profile and blocked him. Then, I pulled up my Contacts and called Leslie.

"Hello?"

"Hey. So, I sent Joel a message when I got home and asked him why he had given me the wrong number."

"Oh my God. I forgot all about Joel with all the stuff that's happened the last few days."

"To be honest, I did too."

"What did he say?"

"Oh, you know, he made a mistake, but since he messed up, he thought we should just stick to the app."

"You always know it's a bad sign when he won't give you his phone number."

"Yeah, the dick probably has a wife."

"Or he's a serial killer."

I sighed. "Really, Leslie?"

"Hey, can you tell me he's not?"

"Well…no," I admitted.

"See."

"Leslie."

"Okay, okay. You're probably right. He's probably married."

"Thank you." I thought I'd just wanted to know I wasn't totally off in my thinking.

"And a serial killer," she added quickly.

She'd just had to slip that in there.

"I'm going to hang up now," I said.

"No, wait."

"What?"

"What did he text you?"

I was confused. "I already told you."

"Not him. Cal."

"Oh." I smiled. "He asked me what I'd been thinking about in our little meeting because I turned red and couldn't sit still."

"What were you thinking about?"

"Sex."

Leslie burst out laughing. "And what did you tell him?"

"Sex." Close enough. I didn't want to say out loud what I had written.

"Oh my God, what did he say?"

I smiled. "He told me I couldn't write stuff like that at work because it made him hard and he wanted to bend me over the desk."

Leslie squealed. "That is so hot. No wonder you told Joel good riddance."

"But it's not like Cal and I are dating."

"But you do realize that you'd rather have someone like Cal rather than Joel, right?"

"Yes. But I'm trying to stay away from alpha males. Or more alpha-like males."

"Then, stay away from Cal."

"Why?"

"Today, when I told him I was your best friend and I knew what had happened between the two of you, he looked me dead in the eye and asked if we were going to have a problem. I might not feel the attraction to him that you do, but I swear a shiver went up my spine. He seems nice, but he's no beta male. He'll do what he needs to do to get the job done."

A shiver went up my spine, too, as I pictured the two of them facing off. I liked it. It also made me slightly jealous. I didn't like that feeling as much.

"Besides, no other man is going to come over to some stranger's house like he did and fuck her the way he fucked you."

"I don't know. My brother would totally show up at some random chick's house if she said she wanted to have sex."

"Yeah, and then your brother would just stand there, waiting for her to make the move."

"Okay, so I've never seen my brother in that situation, but I could totally picture it."

My brother was a little on the dorky side and not a lady's man in the least.

"And was Cal like that?"

"No. He pushed me against the wall and kissed me."

"Yes. That is what I'm talking about."

"When's the last time you got laid?"

Leslie sighed. "Too long. Asher's out of town."

I laughed.

"What's so funny?"

"My sweet, sweet Leslie is saving herself for her boyfriend," I teased.

"He's not my boyfriend."

"Yet you're not dating or having sex with anyone else."

"Shut up, boss-fucker."

I laughed harder.

"You just wait, Indy. Some guy is going to make an honest woman out of you too."

"I can only hope. Unlike some people, I don't want to be single forever."

"I have to go."

"Leslie, don't leave me. I need you," I cried out.

"I'm going to hack into your phone and text Cal and tell him you want him to come over right now."

"You wouldn't. Besides, you don't know how to hack a phone."

"But I know someone who can."

"You still wouldn't. You love me too much."

"You're right; I do. But I'm very tempted."

"Listen, I really do have to go."

"Same. Will you let me know if you hear from Cal again?"

"Duh. Like you have to ask."

"Later, Indy."

"Bye, Leslie."

After hanging up, I made myself dinner and cleaned up the kitchen. I did some things around the house before I let myself sit down and relax with my phone.

I'd told myself not to look because I didn't have a notification, but I checked my messages anyway, just to see if Cal had texted me.

I really wanted to know what he had been thinking about during our introductory meeting. For all I knew, he'd just said that to get me interested. And this was why I needed to get away from alpha males.

I watched an episode of a show I'd found on Netflix, read a few chapters in a book, texted back and forth with Leslie, and spent way too much time on social media.

I had just brushed my teeth and climbed into bed when my phone dinged. Figuring it was Leslie and that she could wait to talk tomorrow, I almost didn't answer it.

But curiosity got the better of me, and I picked up my phone. I mean, what if something exciting had happened to my best friend and I missed it because I was too lazy to look at my phone?

But it wasn't Leslie.

Cal: Do you still want an answer to your question? It's not going to be pretty.

I knew exactly what question he was talking about. It was the one where I'd asked what he wanted to do to me while I was in his office.

My heartbeat picked up, and electricity raced through my body.

Me: Yes.

As if he even needs to ask.

Cal: I imagined you getting on your knees and crawling under my desk to suck my cock. Then, after I came down your throat, I'd pick you up and spread you on top of it, so I could eat that beautiful pussy of yours. After making you come once, maybe twice, I'd bury myself inside you so far, you'd cry out in pain. But then I'd fuck away all the hurt—to the point you'd forget how rough I was with you.

When I finished reading his message, my eyes were wide, and I was stunned. I immediately went back up to the top and read it again.

And again.

Leslie was right about this guy being an alpha male, and I found it extremely hot.

NINE
CAL

I WAITED for Indy to text me back, but after a few seconds, I figured it wasn't going to happen. I'd warned her that my thoughts weren't pretty.

I locked my screen and got out of my vehicle. Instead of thinking about my hot employee, I really should be going to bed or at least looking at the work I'd brought home.

I'd gone to my parents' house for dinner, thinking I would be there a couple of hours and then come home and work.

I hadn't planned on my brother and sister being there with their spouses and kids. All the people, including three small children, in the house made for a long night. I'd also accidentally seen my sister-in-law's boob when she was breastfeeding. My brother had just shrugged and moved on.

It was going to take some getting used to, having so much family around.

I walked into my dark house and took a minute to enjoy the silence. I loved my family, but they could be a lot. I was grateful my cousin Sloan had found me a place that was close enough to visit when I wanted but far enough away that they wouldn't be poking their heads in my front door every day.

I threw my phone on the kitchen counter and walked to my bedroom to change. I pulled on a pair of gray sweatpants and a white T-shirt because if I was going to work this late, I was going to be comfortable. Back in the living room, I turned on the ten o'clock news and opened my laptop.

I didn't get very far into my work when my phone buzzed against my counter.

> Indy: I've typed out several messages, and I just keep deleting them.

I frowned. I had no idea what she meant by that.

> Me: Not everyone likes bluntness. I apologize for what I wrote even if it was true.

> Me: I take that back. I apologize if I offended you. But I'm not going to say I'm sorry for wanting what I want.

> Indy: No, I'm not offended.

> Me: That's good. But was it too much? Are you going to HR?

I was joking about the last part, but when she didn't reply, I feared she was going to say yes. I wasn't going to apologize for wanting her, but maybe I should be careful about getting involved with someone who could get me fired.

It took her so long to reply that I set my phone down

and went back to work. When my phone buzzed again, I almost didn't answer because I didn't feel like playing games. I wanted her to just come out and write what she was thinking.

Indy: Are you a dom?

Me: A dom?

Indy: A dominant. Are you into BDSM?

Indy: Because I'm not a submissive.

A grin spread across my face. Now, I understood why it had taken her so long to respond.

Me: No, I'm not a dom, and I don't practice BDSM. Not really anyway.

Indy: What does "not really" mean?

Me: Like I said, I'm not a dominant, but I do like to be in charge in the bedroom. Not always, but often. Also, I've never used whips or floggers, but I don't think a light spanking has ever hurt anyone. And if you've never been tied up and tortured into orgasm, you don't know what you're missing. But that's the extent of my BDSM, which is why I said I don't practice it.

Indy: How is being in charge different than being a dom?

Me: Are you quizzing me? Is this a test?

Indy: No, I'm just curious.

Me: Let's say you and I were in bed together. I might choose to push you on the bed, roll you over, and take you from behind. But if it's not something you want, I wouldn't force you. I don't want to control you. And I'm definitely not into the humiliation thing that some doms practice on their subs. Not judging anyone who is. Everyone has their own kinks. It's just not for me.

Indy: What if I want to humiliate you?

I laughed out loud. This was the first hint of flirting I'd seen since I texted her my lewd message.

Me: Haha-haha. No.

Indy: LOL. Okay then.

Me: Are these questions the reason you didn't know how to answer?

Indy: Yes.

Me: Did it turn you off?

Indy: No. The opposite in fact.

I groaned.

Me: Are you wet right now?

Indy: Yes. Are you hard?

Me: I am now.

Indy: Good. You should suffer as much as me.

Me: You could touch yourself.

Indy: So could you.

Me: It's not as much fun.

Indy: Have you ever noticed there are way more sex toys for women than men?

Me: I've honestly never thought about it, but I assume it has to do with the number of women who go unsatisfied. It's not hard for a man to bring himself to orgasm.

Indy: That's probably it.

Me: Does this mean you're going to use a toy on yourself?

I closed my eyes and pictured her pleasuring herself.

My cock was starting to ache, which was not conducive to getting work done. I really needed to end this conversation before I lost the last ounce of motivation I had to get through the spreadsheets staring at me from my computer.

Indy: That depends.

Me: On what?

I had no control. My dick and primitive brain were in charge now.

Indy: On if you come over or not.

Damn it all to hell.

Me: I'll be there in fifteen minutes.

TEN

INDY

I JUMPED out of bed and ran to the bathroom to put on some mascara. I didn't bother with a full face of makeup, but my eyes were going to look good when Cal came over. I also ran a brush through my hair, so it wasn't a mess in the back from where I'd been lying on my pillow.

Next, I went through my drawers to find a pair of cute pajamas. I wasn't going to go full sexy because I didn't want him to think I'd gotten dressed for him. Men already had big enough egos without women feeding into them.

But I was not going to let him show up here with me in my shirt with a hole from where the seam had come apart in the armpit. It had been a favorite of mine since high school and so comfortable. I refused to get rid of it, and I was too lazy to sew up the rip. And my bottoms had a couple of paint stains on them from where I'd brushed against a drying wall after I painted my bedroom. Like my shirt, they were comfortable and one of my favorites but not something I wanted Cal to see me in.

My doorbell rang about five minutes later, and I opened the door, grabbed Cal's shirt, and pulled him inside.

I hated to admit it, but he was the perfect man for me in the bedroom. I loved it when a man took charge, but I had no desire to be anyone's submissive. I loved reading about BDSM, but in real life, I didn't like being controlled. It was the same reason I'd never joined the military. I didn't think I would have been able to keep my mouth shut when the drill instructor started yelling at me, telling me what to do.

Cal smiled at me, kicked the door closed behind him, and threw me over his shoulder.

I started laughing. "What are you doing?"

"Carrying you to the bedroom." I could hear the smile in his voice.

"I can walk."

"But this is more fun."

When we got to my bedroom, Cal put me down on the bed. "Do you still have the box of condoms I brought over?"

I nodded toward my nightstand. "In the top drawer."

"Is that where you keep your sex toys too?"

I sat up and leaned back on my hands, eyebrows raised. "I never said I had sex toys."

Cal opened the drawer, pulled out the condoms, and plopped them on the nightstand. "Honey, you didn't have to say it."

I bit my lip. "What are you going to do with them?"

He laughed. "Depends on what it is, but I thought you'd figured out that I was going to use them on you."

I looked down at the bulge in front of his gray sweatpants. "I don't think I need a toy when you're packing that thing."

R.L. KENDERSON

Cal laughed and sauntered over to me. I sat up straight and moved closer to him, and then he lifted my chin and kissed me.

He cupped my face at first in an almost-tender way before he slid a hand down and over my breast. He played with my hard nipple until I was writhing on the bed. Then, he stepped back and pulled off his shirt, and I did the same with mine.

He came back to the bed and nudged me to my back as he kissed me. His lips traveled down my neck and over my breast where he licked and sucked on my nipple. I grabbed the back of his head and scratched at his scalp with my nails.

I was ready to get fully naked with him.

To let him know I was all good with foreplay and ready for him to get inside me, I grabbed for his cock.

I never wanted to be a woman who said size mattered, but I was totally impressed with his thickness and his length. It was probably more that he knew how to use his equipment, but the size didn't hurt either.

As soon as I touched his shaft, Cal stood up and moved away from me.

"What are you doing?"

He smirked. "Tell me where the toys are, Indy."

I stuck out my lower lip. "But I don't need a toy. I have you."

He grinned. "Thanks for the ego boost. I know you don't need it, but I want it."

It was silly because I was pretty adventurous in the bedroom, but the truth was, I had never used a toy with anyone but myself. And for some reason, just thinking about it made me embarrassed. It was one thing to have a guy pleasuring me while he was also getting pleasure, but it was another for him to put his sole focus on me. What if I made a stupid face or squirted all over him?

I realized that I most likely made ridiculous expressions when a guy went down on me, but I thought the fact that he was below my belly button and I could hide my face from him made it different.

"I'm not telling," I said.

Cal shook his head in disappointment and picked up his shirt from my floor.

"What are you doing?" I cried out as he pulled his tee over his head.

"Getting dressed."

"I can see that. But why?"

"I want to play, and you don't. It's best I leave."

I studied his face. He looked serious, but I could see a tiny sparkle in his eye.

"Please don't."

"Why not?"

"Because I want to come."

He strolled over to me, kissed me deep, and pulled away. "That's exactly what I want for you too." He lifted an eyebrow. "Are you going to give up the goods?"

"Why are you pushing this?" I whispered, genuinely curious.

"Because I know you want to. You're just afraid to admit it."

I turned away from his gaze. "What if I do something weird, like come all over you?"

He put a finger under my chin and raised my face until I

met his eyes. "Do you always squirt when you use your toys?"

"Not always, but sometimes."

He closed his eyes and took a deep breath. When he opened them again, he said, "Then, I'm definitely not touching you until you tell me where they are. Even if I have to go home and jerk off all night."

I smiled and held my breath. "They're in the bottom drawer, under where the condoms were," I said before I lost my resolve and changed my mind.

He laughed. "I should have known." He knelt down and opened my bottom drawer. Right in front was my favorite vibrator. He picked it up. "What do we have here?"

"It's a clitoral vibrator," I said. It was small enough to fit in my hand and had two little fingers on it to go on each side of my clit, which I really, really liked.

He turned to me. "You like this one, don't you?"

I shrugged. "It's probably my favorite."

He shook his head. "It's probably your favorite? Liar. It is your favorite." He pulled out another one that looked more like a dildo.

"That one is okay. I don't care for it."

He didn't question me, just picked up another one.

We went through a few more until there weren't any more, except the one I had shoved in the back.

"Well, well, well, what do we have here? This one is wrapped up in a towel," he said as he pulled out my Magic Wand.

The thing was huge. The head was the size of a tennis ball.

Cal grinned. "The Cadillac of vibrators."

I shook my head. "Nope. Not going to happen. I've never used that one."

He chuckled, closed the drawer, and stood.

My eyes opened wide. "What are you doing?"

"Why do you have this if you've never used it?"

I rolled my eyes. "Leslie bought it for me after a particularly bad breakup. She told me I would never need a man again after using it."

Hint, hint. I wanted him to think I might not need him if he used it on me.

Cal threw it on the bed. "Good to know. But I'm guessing there are women everywhere who still go on to date after using this beast."

"Are you sure you want to risk it?"

He laughed and grabbed the hem of my pants. "Hell yeah, I do."

Cal took off all his clothes, slid on a condom, and got on the bed. He pushed my legs up as he thrust inside me. After a few strokes, I had my eyes shut, and I was clutching at his legs.

I was getting lost in the sensation of him moving inside me, floating in my body, that I didn't even hear the Magic Wand being turned on.

When he put it between my legs, my eyes flew open, and I instinctively tried to put my legs down.

Cal used his free hand to keep one of my legs back, so I was open to him. "Shh…it's okay. I've got you."

It was like a jackhammer had hit my clit, and I finally understood why Leslie had bought it for me. I thought I was going to set the fastest record for coming.

"Oh shit."

"That's it, Indy, just sit back and enjoy the ride."

My legs began to shake, and I couldn't control them, but I tried not to think about anything but Cal's deep strokes inside me and the vibrations on my clit.

A huge wave flushed across my body as my middle cramped up. I felt my vagina close around Cal's shaft, and an almost fullness inside me exploded.

When I couldn't take any more, I reached toward Cal and swatted his hand away. He chuckled as he turned the vibrator off.

I tried to open my eyes and turn my face up, but I was too weak. Cal dropped his body over my own and nuzzled my neck.

"Am I still alive?" I asked.

"Damn right you are. I can still feel you pulsing around me. Pretty sure dead girls don't do that."

I took in his words and could feel the same thing now that I was paying attention to it.

"Did I squirt?" I asked.

"Damn right you did. It was the best thing I've ever seen. I think every woman needs one of those things."

I opened my eyes and turned to face him. "And a man who knows how to use it on her," I added.

"Damn right," he said.

ELEVEN
INDY

WEDNESDAY MORNING, I woke up to an empty bed with a note on my nightstand.

Left early to change for work. See you there.
Cal
P.S. No playing with the Magic Wand without me.

I smiled and rolled over. Even though it was hump day, I felt too good to be bummed about going to work.

I hadn't told Leslie that Cal had come over again last night, so I did my best to act normal when I got to work in the morning. I wasn't going to keep it from her, but I was going to wait until we could go to lunch.

"You're being weird today," Leslie said as we took our morning break.

I frowned. "I am?" I didn't think I had done anything unusual.

"Uh, yeah. Patrick came over and yelled at us this morning, and you just shrugged your shoulders at him and said, 'Okay.'"

I lifted a shoulder. "I didn't feel like arguing with him again. We'll get it done by Friday. He'll just have to wait."

Truth was, I was in a good mood and didn't want Patrick to ruin it.

"But you love arguing with Patrick."

"No, I don't. You like arguing with him."

Leslie smiled. "Okay, maybe. But it's usually when I'm feeling sexually frus—" She gasped.

My eyes widened. "Shh," I said.

We weren't alone in the break room, and our coworker Stu was sitting in the corner, but I wasn't taking any chances that he might hear us.

"Were you going to tell me?" she said in an almost whisper.

"Of course I was. I was waiting until lunch."

"Whew. You're forgiven," she joked.

We both laughed when Cal walked into the break room and headed for the coffeemaker.

"Hello, ladies," he said to Leslie and me. "Hello, Stu," he said to the only other person in the room.

"Hello, Cal," Leslie said a little too seductively.

I kicked her under the table.

The corner of Cal's mouth went up, but he basically ignored Leslie's comment.

Meanwhile, I shot dagger eyes at my friend. I loved her, but sometimes, she liked to make waves where none needed to be made.

Leslie grinned at me and turned in her seat. "So, Cal, how is Minnesota treating you?"

Cal poured his coffee, turned around, and took a sip. "Good. I have to get used to being around my family again." He lifted his brow. "They can be a little much sometimes."

"Oh?" I asked. I was curious about the new boss and my sex partner.

"Yeah. My parents invited me over for dinner last evening but didn't tell me that my brother and sister were coming with their spouses and kids. I was worn out by the end of the night." He took another drink and smiled behind his cup. "It's a good thing I found some energy after I got home because there were a couple of other things I needed to take care of last night."

I had taken a drink of my Diet Pepsi at the same time he said the last sentence and swallowed my pop wrong. I started coughing and couldn't stop.

My new boss was evil.

Leslie smirked across from me.

She wasn't much better.

"Are you okay?" Leslie asked.

I held up a hand. "I'll…I'll survive."

"Mr. Callan," Keith said from the doorway.

"Yes?"

Keith looked down at his tablet. "I confirmed your flight for tomorrow at six fifteen in the morning. You'll need to get to the airport by four thirty, so you can make it through security."

Cal held up his hand. "Yes, I know the two-hour rule."

That was especially true with our Minneapolis–St. Paul

airport. I really liked our airport as far as cleanliness, restaurants, and shops, but the security lines were brutal.

"But I have TSA PreCheck status," Cal finished.

I didn't know why I was surprised. Maybe because the guy who'd come to my house was in sweats and a T-shirt and his hair had been finger-combed.

The guy in front of me was dressed in nice slacks and a dress shirt, and every hair was in place. This was the guy who had precheck status.

Keith wasn't impressed though. "You should still be there by five a.m."

Cal nodded and smiled politely. "Will do."

Leslie turned in her seat again. "So, where are you going?"

I was so glad she'd asked because I was dying to know, but I felt like it was overstepping if I asked because we'd slept with each other. I didn't want him to think I was getting attached to him. I didn't know if he was one of those guys who thought women couldn't have sex without falling in love.

News flash: Us women totally could.

Cal sighed. "I'm flying to New York to take care of a few things before I move away completely. Then, on Sunday, I'm flying to Chicago for a week. The board wants me there for some training."

"What are we going to do without a boss?" I joked.

Cal pulled out his cell phone and looked at the screen. "The Chicago office is sending a replacement while I'm there."

"I wasn't serious," I said. "We can survive without you."

He smiled apologetically. "Sorry, I have to take this." He

headed for the door. "This is Callan," he said, answering his phone.

Stu got up right behind him, threw his trash away, and left with a quick goodbye.

"This sucks," Leslie said. "We just got a new boss, and now, they're going to take him away and send another new person."

I nodded my head in agreement.

"Did you know he was leaving?" Leslie asked.

"No."

"Uh-oh."

I waved my hand in the air. "We're not dating. He doesn't have to tell me anything."

And he didn't, but a small part of me couldn't help wondering what was going to happen between Cal and me while he was gone. A big part of me didn't even know what I wanted to happen.

I guessed I'd have to wait to find out. Until then, I wasn't going to worry about it. Cal was one man in a city of over four million people. I certainly didn't need him.

TWELVE

INDY

THURSDAY WAS A NORMAL DAY. On Friday, I went over to my parents' for dinner along with my sister, who was also single. Then, Saturday, I had plans with Leslie, her boyfriend, and his friend.

Leslie had begged me to go on a food and brewery tour in downtown Minneapolis. She and Asher had wanted to go for a long time, but the place required a minimum of four people to be booked for the tour to operate. Supposedly, they had a good reason—they didn't want to waste gas on a small party or something—but I couldn't quite remember what it was now. I knew I was only getting dragged along so that Leslie and Asher could go on this tour.

The tour was a thing where we all got on a bus, drove around the city, and stopped at various bars to eat their food and drink their alcohol. I really couldn't complain too much about being asked to go because I liked food and I liked drinks.

I was supposed to arrive fifteen minutes early, and I made it just in time.

I could see the worried expression on Leslie's face as she scanned the room for me.

"Leslie," I called out.

She spun around and grinned when she saw me. "You're here."

"I am."

She hugged me when I reached her.

"Hey, Asher," I said to Leslie's tall, dark, and handsome boyfriend—or non-boyfriend, according to her.

He was about six-four, muscular with golden brown skin, and had almost black eyes that were warm and genuinely happy to see me. I really liked Asher, and I thought Leslie was nuts for denying him official boyfriend status.

"Hey, Indy," he said as he gave me a one-armed hug. "How are you?"

"Oh, good. And you? When did you get back into town?"

"Wednesday."

I smiled knowingly at Leslie. "So, that explains why I got two one-worded texts from you on Wednesday night."

Leslie rolled her eyes. "No comment."

Asher dropped his arm from me and put it around Leslie. "Aw…my girl is shy."

I burst out laughing. "That's the funniest thing I've heard all day. She's anything but shy."

Leslie stuck her tongue out at me.

"Ash," someone called from across the room, and the three of us looked up.

"Hey, Marcus," Ash yelled back.

I looked at Leslie. "You didn't tell me that Marcus was

the friend coming. You wouldn't have had to drag me here then."

She shrugged. "I didn't know or I would have told you."

Marcus was probably my favorite friend of Asher's. We got along great and always had fun together.

When Marcus reached us, he and Asher did their usual fancy handshake. Then, he hugged Leslie and me.

"Hey, ladies." Marcus had short, dark hair, brown eyes, and tan skin. I had always thought he was hot, but he'd had a girlfriend since I'd known him.

I pushed my hip into Marcus's. "Hey back. Long time no see."

He held out his arms. "Now, we have the next three hours to make up for that."

"I hope we get really drunk." I looked around. "I mean, I hope I get really drunk."

"Man trouble?" Asher asked.

"No, not really. I don't know if Leslie told you about the guy I was seeing, but he gave me someone else's phone number." I gave a double thumbs-down sign.

"Ouch," Asher said.

"Meh." I shrugged. "I don't think I liked him that much because when I blocked him, I didn't feel anything. Except maybe disappointment at wasting my time."

"He doesn't know what he's missing," Leslie said.

"She's right," Marcus agreed.

"Thanks, guys."

A colorful bus pulled up outside the building.

"I think that's our ride," Asher said.

I rubbed my hands together. "Let's do this."

By the time the tour was over, we all had full stomachs and a decent alcohol buzz.

"That was fun," I admitted.

"It wasn't too bad," Marcus agreed. "Thanks for inviting me."

Asher punched Marcus in the arm. "I hope it took your mind off Veronica."

"Oh no, what happened with Veronica?" I asked.

"They're on a break," Leslie said.

Asher looked at his watch. "It's only nine p.m. Do you guys want to do something else?"

Marcus shrugged. "I'm game."

I checked my phone. I didn't know what I had expected to see, but nothing was there. "Sure. I'm in."

"We should pick somewhere we can walk," Leslie suggested.

I hiccuped. "Excellent idea."

Everyone laughed at me.

We walked to the nearest nightclub. We weren't dressed up like most of the people there since we had dressed for riding around in a bus, but I didn't really care. It was more comfortable to be in jeans rather than a short skirt anyway.

"Do you want something to drink?" Marcus asked me as Leslie and Asher took off somewhere.

"Yes, please." I put my arm in his. "Don't leave me, okay? Since it looks like our friends have ditched us."

He patted my hand. "I've got you."

"So, what happened with Veronica?" I asked as we waited for drinks. Our bodies were close in the crowded area, and I could feel his body heat. I also noticed how good he smelled. "Or do you not want to talk about it?"

He shrugged. "I honestly don't know. But Leslie's wrong. We're more than just on a break. Veronica moved all her stuff out two weekends ago."

"I'm sorry."

"Thanks, but I think it's for the best. We'd been dating for nearly ten years."

"Damn, you were almost married."

The bartender brought our beverages, and Marcus took a long drink. "One would think, but she always said she wasn't ready. Truth was, I wasn't ready either. At least, not with her. It's best we called it quits when we did instead of forcing marriage."

I squeezed his upper arm, noting the muscles underneath my hand. "That sucks."

"You're right; it does." He set his finished drink on the bar. "That's why we should go and dance. We're supposed to be having fun."

I lifted my glass. "To exes."

Marcus grinned and raised his empty tumbler. "To exes."

I tilted my head back and finished my glass. "Let's go and dance like we're single."

Marcus laughed and held out his arm. "Lead the way."

THIRTEEN

CAL

"CALLAN, are you ready to get your ass to the bar? What is taking you so long?"

I popped my head out of my friend Jack's bathroom. "I'm almost done. I have to finish getting pretty," I joked.

"You were born pretty, dude. Hurry up. Everyone's waiting for us."

I walked out and down the hall. "Okay, okay. I'm coming."

Jack raised a brown eyebrow. "I would hope so. This is your goodbye party."

After being in Minnesota for almost two months, I was excited to see and say goodbye to all my New York friends. I didn't regret moving, even with my complaints about my family, but I was going to miss my friends.

"Let's get out of here," I said.

I was staying at Jack's apartment, and he had picked a bar that was close to his place, so we could walk there and home. When we strolled through the door, a bunch of people started cheering, and a grin broke across my face.

"Cal, Cal, Cal," they started chanting, and I pushed my hands down in a motion to tell them to lower their voices.

After they all quieted, I said, "Thanks, everyone, for being here. I'm glad you could all come out." I clapped my hands together. "Now, who's buying me my first drink?"

Everyone laughed, and a hand shot up in the back. "I will."

The crowd parted, and there stood my ex-girlfriend, Autumn. We'd dated for over four years, and we hadn't had a pretty breakup. I was surprised to see she was there.

She sauntered over to me, her blue eyes bright. "Do you still drink whiskey?"

I grinned. "You know it."

She nodded toward the bar. "Let's go then."

I walked with her to get drinks. "I didn't think I'd see you here," I told her honestly.

"I heard that you had moved, and I was a little sad you hadn't said goodbye. So, when Jack invited me to your going-away party, I figured it was my chance."

We were close, standing at the bar with people all around us.

"I didn't think you cared if you ever saw me again."

The bartender came over and leaned in to get each of our orders, and then he disappeared.

She arched up and spoke in my ear, "You should know better than that, Cal. We were together for years."

The bar wasn't so loud that she had to speak directly in my ear, and it didn't take a genius to realize she was flirting with me. I did have my doubts since we'd had a less than amicable breakup, but when she pushed her breasts against my arm, I knew for sure she wanted me.

I leaned down to her ear this time. "What's your game?" I asked.

She pulled back. "No game. I just want to give you a nice goodbye."

I laughed. *I just bet you do.* "Where's Victor?"

She shook her blonde hair out and looked away. "We broke up."

"I'm sorry. I couldn't hear you." I wasn't sure I had gotten that. I wanted her to say it again because Victor was the guy she'd left me for.

"We broke up," she repeated, looking at me this time.

"That's too bad." And I meant it.

The bartender brought over our drinks, but I saw the surprised look on her face out of the corner of my eye. That just showed how much she didn't know me. I wasn't going to shove it in her face or gloat.

"Thanks," she said.

I cocked my head toward some friends. "I'll talk to you later. Thanks again for coming."

"Later," she said disappointedly as I walked away.

I found Jack and another friend of ours named Voss.

"Was that your ex you were talking to?" Voss asked.

I took a drink of my whiskey. "Yep. Autumn broke up with Victor."

Jack rolled his eyes. "And now, she what? Wants a goodbye fuck?"

If I had to guess by the way she had been flirting, I'd have to say yes. "I don't know. Or she wants to get back together."

"Too bad for her, you live half a country away," Jack said.

"More like, thank God," Voss corrected. "She was not good for you. I'm glad you broke up."

I had to agree with them. Autumn and I had fought a lot when we were together, and while I hadn't seen it at the time, it was a good thing she'd broken up with me.

"I'm done talking about her though. I want to see who else is here."

INDY

Marcus led me out to the dance floor. At first, we danced around each other, but with every song, we moved closer and closer until we were dirty-dancing so hard that we could be in the movie.

I was hot and sweaty and needed another drink, but I was having a lot of fun. It didn't hurt that Marcus was sexy and a good dancer. His ex-girlfriend was crazy for breaking up with him.

His hand moved down my back and cupped my ass. He brought my lower body closer to his, and I sighed when I felt his erection.

"Too much?" he asked.

"No," I said, but I wasn't as happy as I should be.

He pulled me even closer, and I wrapped my arms around his neck. I'd liked this guy for years, and now, he was giving me attention. I should be more excited, yet something was off.

I hoped I wasn't broken.

A couple ran into us, breaking us apart. They were

drunk and both apologized profusely. I wanted to tell them *thank you* because I had begun to feel awkward, being that close to Marcus.

Then, it hit me.

We'd been in the friend zone for way too long, and I couldn't see him as anything other than that now. I bet he felt the same way; he just didn't know it.

"Do you mind if we get off the floor?" I asked. "I think I might have twisted my ankle a tad," I lied so we'd both have an out.

"Oh, yes. Are you okay? Do you need help?"

I smiled and shook my head. "No, it's not that bad. I just don't think I should keep dancing on it."

"I understand."

We walked toward the front door and ran into Leslie and Asher.

"You two are still alive?" I said.

"I'm sorry. I tried calling you." Leslie waved her phone at us.

"We were dancing. I couldn't hear anything." I found my phone, and sure enough, I had some missed calls. "At least we found you now. I think I'm going to call it a night."

"Already?" Asher asked. "It's only eleven."

"Yeah, a couple people ran into us on the dance floor. Kind of ruined the mood."

"I understand." Leslie gave me a hug. "Are you going to be okay out there?"

"I'll walk her," Marcus offered.

"You don't have to leave on account of me."

He shrugged. "It's fine."

The two of us said goodbye to Leslie and Asher and headed back to where we'd parked our cars.

"You really didn't have to leave, you know," I said. "I have pepper spray in my purse."

"It's okay. I didn't feel like being the third wheel to those two."

I nodded. I understood that.

We walked in silence until we reached the bar where we'd met up at the beginning of the night.

"Here's my car. Thanks for making sure I made it safely."

"You're welcome. You're okay to drive?"

"Yes. I only had one drink at the club." I didn't even have a buzz because I had danced it off.

He smiled. "I just had to make sure."

I unlocked my door, and Marcus took a step closer.

"Can I ask you a question?" he asked.

"Sure."

"Is it okay if I ask you out sometime? We can start with coffee or go straight to dinner."

I nodded. "I think I'd like that."

He smiled at me. I hadn't realized how nervous he'd been about asking me. I couldn't help it; it made me feel good about myself.

"I'll call you then."

"Sounds good." I got in my car and waved goodbye.

Hopefully, I'd feel less awkward on our date than I had tonight.

FOURTEEN
CAL

"YOU LOOK DRUNK, CAL."

I leaned back on the barstool and saw it was Autumn who had taken the seat next to mine. "That's because I am drunk."

"You also look sad. I don't remember you being a sad drunk."

"I'm not a sad drunk. I'm drunk *and* sad." I looked around the half-empty bar. "This is the last time I might ever see some of these people."

She put her hand on mine. "I suppose you've lived here a long time."

"Over ten years."

She chuckled. "I know how long you've lived here. We dated, remember?"

I pointed a finger at her. "Right."

"Can I give you something that will make you feel better?"

I studied her. I was drunk, as in I couldn't drive. I wasn't falling-down, pissing-on-myself drunk.

"Autumn, we're not doing this."

"Not doing what?"

"We're not having sex."

"Who said anything about sex?"

I shrugged. "Okay then. Show me what you have for me."

She stood and nodded her head toward the back hall-way. "Come with me."

I snorted but got off my own stool.

She grabbed my hand and drew me to the back of the bar.

"You're not planning on jumping me, are you? Because I only have about ten bucks on me and no credit cards."

"I'm not going to rob you," she said over her shoulder.

We walked into the hall, passing the women's restroom, the men's restroom, and a door that said *Employees Only*.

She led me all the way to the back where it said *Emergency Exit—Alarm Will Sound* before she stopped, pushed me against the wall, and kissed me.

I kissed her back for a few seconds before I ripped my mouth away. "Autumn, I already said, we're not doing this."

She cupped my shaft through my pants. "That's not what Mr. Happy says."

"I never liked you calling my dick that name, even when we were dating."

She kissed me again and stuck out her lower lip. "Please, Cal. You're moving away, and I'll probably never see you again." She squeezed my cock. "And I miss this thing. I forgot how big you are."

I pulled her hand away. "I said no, Autumn."

"Why? Do you have a girlfriend?"

An image of Indy popped into my head. "No, I don't have a girlfriend. But if you have to tell yourself I do, then by all means, go for it."

"You used to be more fun."

I shrugged. "I guess I did." Why she thought that was an insult and might change my mind, I had no idea. "I don't have a condom anyway."

She smiled. "That's okay. You can take me bare."

I gently pushed her away. "And I'm out."

I headed back to the bar, Autumn's high heels clicking behind me.

"Most guys love having sex without a condom. We've done it before."

I stopped and turned so fast that she almost ran into me. "Yeah, back when we were dating. You and I broke up two years ago."

She put her hand on her hip. "Are you saying I'm dirty?"

It was really hard for me not to walk away. It was only because she had meant something to me at one point that I didn't. "No, and I don't appreciate you twisting my words like that. I expect better from you."

She started crying.

"What did I say now?"

She cried harder.

I pulled her into my arms. "I'm sorry. That was very insensitive of me." I rubbed her back and let her cover my shirt in her tears until she calmed down some.

I drew her away from me.

"I'm sorry," she said.

"It's okay. Something is obviously upsetting you. But if it's because I won't have sex with you, trust me, I'm not worth it." I smiled. "I mean, I know I'm good in bed, but I'm not the only one out there."

She gave me a wobbly smile for a second and went back to being sad. "I'm pregnant."

"What?" I looked at the bar. "But you were drinking."

She shook her head. "Club soda."

"What do I say? Congratulations? It'll be okay?"

She shrugged. "I'm pregnant, and Victor broke up with me."

"What a prick." I looked back down the hall. "Is that why you said we could have sex without a condom?"

She turned red and didn't answer.

"Autumn, were you trying to have sex with me, so you could pass the baby off as mine?"

She didn't say yes, but she didn't say no.

I ran a hand through my hair. "Autumn, that is fucked up."

"I know, okay? But I'm desperate."

"Give me your phone."

She suspiciously eyed me. "Why?"

"Just give me the phone." I motioned her to hurry up with my hand.

She unlocked it for me and handed it over, and I scrolled until I found Victor's name.

> Me as Autumn: We need to talk. This baby is half yours, and I didn't make him on my own. That's fine if you want nothing to do with him, but you are paying child support. And you're the one who's going to have to look him in the eyes someday when he finds you as an adult and explain to him how you were a selfish piece of shit.

> This is your chance to turn it around. I'll be waiting for your call.

I handed the cell back to Autumn, and she gasped when she saw the text I'd sent.

"I can't believe you did that."

"I don't like seeing my friends hurt."

She smiled. "We're friends?"

"Yeah, we're friends."

She looked at her phone again. "Do you think he'll respond?"

"If he knows what's good for him."

"Can I call you if I ever need more advice? Like, from a guy's point of view."

"Sure." I took her phone again and put in my new Minnesota number.

"You're really serious about not coming back," she said when she saw that I had changed my number.

"Yes, I am."

"Yo, Cal, you ready to go?" Jack shouted across the open room.

"I'll be there in a sec," I yelled back. I turned back to Autumn. "Good luck with the baby and everything."

She held out her hand, and I shook it.

"Same to you, Cal. New York will miss you."

FIFTEEN
INDY

I GOT HOME SAFELY, got ready for bed, and climbed under the covers when my phone beeped.

> Leslie: Did you make it home safe?

> Me: Just crawled into bed. You still out?

> Leslie: No, we're on our way home. Talk tomorrow?

> Me: Of course.

> Leslie: Night.

> Me: Night.

I set my phone down, and it beeped again. I rolled to my side to take a look. Leslie must have forgotten to tell me something.

But it wasn't Leslie.

89

Cal: You up?

Me: Awake but in bed.

Cal: Same.

Me: How's New York?

Cal: Good. I had a going-away party tonight. It was nice to see my friends.

Me: Are you going to miss it there?

It was crazy, but I didn't want him to say yes. I wanted him to like living here.

Cal: I don't think I'm going to miss it as much as I originally thought.

Me: That's good.

Cal: What did you do tonight?

Me: Went on a food and beer tour. Then went out to a club for a bit.

Cal: With Leslie?

I went back and forth on just saying yes or telling him everyone who was there, which was stupid. Cal and I weren't a couple or dating.

> Me: Leslie and her boyfriend, Asher, and then Asher's friend Marcus.

> Cal: Sounds like a double date.

I had no idea what Cal meant by this. He was probably just making conversation, but could he actually be jealous?

I pictured him in my head. He was handsome and could have plenty of women. He didn't have to get jealous over someone he'd already slept with.

> Me: No. I've known Marcus for years. We're friends too. And he's had the same girlfriend for a long time.

For some reason, I kept my mouth shut about Marcus and Veronica breaking up.

> Cal: Was it a fun tour?

> Me: It was. It wasn't the greatest night of my life, but I enjoyed myself.

> Cal: I already knew it wasn't the greatest night of your life.

> Me: How did you know that?

> Cal: Because that was last Saturday.

Last Saturday was when I'd texted him for the first time.

Cal: I'm joking. I'm sure you've had plenty of great nights in your life.

Cal: Just ignore me. I've had a long night.

Me: That doesn't sound good. I thought a going-away party was supposed to be fun.

Cal: It was. I just ran into my ex, and it was a little much.

This news had my heart picking up speed. I didn't like the thought of him being with his ex, and I also really didn't like feeling that way.

Me: I'm sorry about that. What happened?

Cal: Not much. I just hadn't seen her in a long time and was not expecting to talk to her.

I wondered if there was more to the story, but I wasn't going to press.

Me: I can imagine that was awkward. I'd feel the same if one of my exes showed up.

Cal: You don't stay friends with them, I take it?

Me: That's one way to put it. I would like to say I've had amicable breakups, but they always seem to end badly. I think there is something wrong with me. LOL.

Cal: Why would you say that?

Me: I'm the common denominator in all
these relationships.

I'd been waiting so intently for his next text that I wasn't
prepared for the phone to ring, and it scared me.

"Hello?"

"Maybe it's partly you because you always pick the
wrong guys, but it doesn't mean there is something wrong
with you."

I sighed like a teenage girl talking to her crush. This was
the first time we'd talked on the phone. He had a nice voice.
"Thanks. I'm not sure if it's true, but thank you."

"Speaking of exes, you never told me about who you
were trying to message the night I came over. I'm guessing
you're not friends."

I laughed. "I wouldn't say he's my ex either. I met him
on a dating app, we went out a few times, and when I asked
for his phone number, he gave me yours."

"Accident?" Cal asked.

"That's what he claimed when I called him out on it two
days later. But if a woman you're dating says she's going to
text you and you don't hear from her for two days, wouldn't
you wonder what happened?"

Cal chuckled. "I'd like to think I would."

"Exactly. Not only did he give me the wrong number,
but there was also no checking in with me. And it had been
two days. So, I told him to go fuck himself."

Laughter erupted on the other side of the phone. "You
didn't."

"You're right; I didn't. But I wanted to. I basically called him out on his BS and said goodbye. Then, I blocked him."

"I'm glad you did," Cal said, still chuckling. "He doesn't deserve you."

"You don't know me that well, but I appreciate that. For all you know, I could secretly be a black widow, and the reason I'm not friends with any of my exes is because they're all dead."

"Then, if I were the guy you met on the dating app, I'd run away."

I laughed this time. I had expected him to be scared or think I was weird. But no, he'd made a joke. I loved it.

"Nah, he's not worth years in prison."

"So, tell me, Indy, what's your favorite food?"

"My favorite food?" I asked with skepticism.

"Yeah. You told me I don't know you that well, so I'm getting to know you. What's your favorite food?"

I rolled onto my back and began to answer his questions, but I made sure he answered mine in return.

SIXTEEN

INDY

THE WEEK HAD DRAGGED on with Cal gone even though the two of us had texted each other a couple of nights. But there had been no more talking on the phone, and we'd never gotten as deep into our conversations as we had on that Saturday night.

But that didn't stop me from being excited to see him once he got back. He had mentioned that he was going to fly in on the weekend and be at work on Monday morning.

I woke up early, anxious to start the day. After giving up on going back to sleep, I got out of bed. And when I should have been taking the extra time to lounge around, I went through half my closet instead. I wanted to show him what he'd been missing all week.

It was probably stupid, but I couldn't stop myself.

I did manage to hold myself back from putting on too much makeup or doing something extreme with my hair. I didn't need everyone at the office asking me what I was dressed up for.

But it happened anyway. When I got off the elevator, the first person I saw was Angela.

"Hey, Indy."

"Morning."

"You look so pretty today."

"Thanks."

The next person I ran into was Keith. He squinted at me.

"What?"

He waved his pen around in a circle in front of my face. "Something's different about you."

"Nothing's different. I'm the same as I always am."

He shook his head, disbelief on his face. "No. Something's different."

I rolled my eyes. "I don't have time for this," I said and walked around him.

When I reached my desk, Leslie turned around and whistled at me.

I threw my stuff down. "What? What is wrong with me?"

She smiled. "Someone is excited to see the boss man today."

I looked around. Thankfully, no one was close. "Shut up."

"I can't. I'm physically incapable."

"Liar."

She shrugged and leaned forward. "I have to assume that's why you look so sexy today?"

"Sexy?" I looked down at my knee-length black skirt and my red blouse. "I wasn't going for sexy."

"You deny wanting to look good for Cal?"

I lifted my chin. "I can neither confirm nor deny."

She laughed.

"Seriously, do I need to change?"

She raised her eyebrows. "Do you have an extra change of clothes?"

"No," I said, defeated, and dropped into my chair.

"Babe, you look fine. You look amazing in fact."

"But I don't want him to think I dressed up for him," I whined.

"He's worked with you for one week. He doesn't know how you normally dress."

I brightened. "Hey, you're right. I might dress like this all the time."

"You look great today," a female coworker said as she walked past us.

I looked at Leslie. "Except that people won't shut up about me looking different today."

"He's not going to be sitting next to you all day," she pointed out.

"You are so smart. You're on fire with the advice today."

"It's the steady stream of sex I've been getting all week."

"*Leslie.*"

"What?"

"Don't ever let men hear you say that. They have big enough egos as it is."

She pointed at me. "That's so true. It's a steady stream of awesome sex and orgasms." She tapped on her temple. "That should fix men from thinking they are qualified."

I raised my eyebrows at her. "Really?"

"You're right. Most men think they're all God's gift to women."

I laughed as I pulled up my work email. I went through and deleted all the emails that were no longer relevant and then opened the new emails. Right at the top was an email from Callan, Nicholas.

The subject line was, *Back in the office*.

I was pretty sure it was an email to everyone, yet part of me wondered if it was just for me.

There was something fun about having a secret at work. I was certain it was the forbidden aspect. I'd never understood why it was so sexy, but it was.

The email was indeed for all the staff. He thanked his temporary replacement, talked about a few things he'd done while in Chicago, and let us know his agenda for the week and when he'd be out of the office.

The last line of the email was to remind everyone about the upcoming Halloween party that we had every year and to let us know that he was looking forward to attending. It was less than two weeks away.

"Did you read today's email?" I asked Leslie.

"Yeah. What about it?"

"The Halloween party."

"Oh, yeah. I'm excited. I didn't have a date last year, but I do this year." She did a little chair dance. "I already made sure Asher's going to be in town for it. Now, I need to come up with the best couples costume. We're going to win that prize this year if it kills us."

"I'm sure you and your boyfriend will be super cute together, no matter what you wear," I said with the straightest face I could.

"Shut up. He's not my boyfriend."

I laughed. "Whatever you have to tell yourself. But I seriously hope you do steal the prize. We can't let Patrick and his wife win again."

"You and I might need to brainstorm. What are you going as?" She looked in the direction of Cal's office. "Are you going to bring a date?"

The last two years, I had gone with my ex-boyfriend. I wasn't really looking forward to going alone, but I couldn't take my boss as my date. "Probably not. There aren't any prospects—unless I meet someone or a new guy shows up on my dating app. But with the party less than two weeks away, I doubt that's going to happen. I can finally wear my antisocial costume."

My ex almost hadn't gone last year, so I'd suggested that Leslie and I go as a couple. My idea was for her to wear a shirt with all the social media icons on it and butterfly wings. Then, I would wear the same shirt with a no symbol—a red circle with a red diagonal line over them. She would be a social butterfly, and I would be antisocial. I couldn't take credit for the concept since I'd found them online, but I thought it was genius, putting them together like that.

Leslie turned me down flat, and my ex decided to go at the last minute. We wore *I'm with Him* and *I'm with Her* T-shirts with arrows pointing at each other. My ex didn't like dressing up, and this was our compromise. As you can guess, we hadn't even been in the running to win.

This could be my year to try out my idea.

"Or I could bring butterfly wings and the no symbol and switch on and off. I could be my own date."

"Ugh. No, Indy. No one's going to get the costumes.

Also, everyone's going to think you're a loser if you do both, like you can't get a date."

"Why don't you tell me how you really feel?"

"You know I'm only looking out for you. You should ask Marcus to go with you?" she suggested, studying my face as she said it.

"Why would you say that?"

"I know that Marcus and Veronica broke up. I know that you have a crush on him—"

"Had," I corrected. "I stopped having a crush on him a couple years ago."

"Whatever." She dismissively waved her hand in the air. "I also know that he asked if he could take you out on a date sometime."

"He told you?" I was surprised.

"No. He told Asher, and Asher told me."

"Of course."

"So, why not go for it?"

I thought about it, and it was actually a good idea. It was for work, so we wouldn't get too crazy. Plus, Leslie and Asher would be there, so I wouldn't be the only one Marcus knew. And lastly, I wouldn't have to show up alone and feel like Leslie and Asher's third wheel.

"You know, it's not a bad idea."

Leslie beamed. "Right? The four of us will have a lot of fun."

Even if I developed no romantic feelings for Marcus and him for me, she was right. We'd all been friends for years, so we would have fun, no matter what.

"I'll text him tonight." I looked out of the corner of my

eye at Leslie as I turned back to my computer. "Maybe he'll be my antisocial to my social butterfly or vice versa," I said in a haughty voice just to get a rise out of my friend.

Leslie groaned and shook her head. "You do, and Asher and I will pretend like we don't know you."

SEVENTEEN
INDY

AFTER LUNCH, I was deep into my work when Cal came over.

"Hello," he greeted our little group. "How are you all today?"

He met each one of our eyes, and when he got to me, his eyes didn't stray to my outfit, for which I was grateful. Everyone was watching him, and they all would have noticed him checking me out.

Or maybe Leslie had been right, and he thought today was how I always dressed. I had only gotten two more comments on my look that morning, so I could have been freaking myself out when I first got to work.

"We're good," one of the members of our team said.

"My replacement didn't give you a hard time? No complaints?"

We all shook our heads. We'd barely seen the woman.

"She was pretty much in her office the whole time," Patrick said as he walked up to join us.

"Hmm," Cal said with a frown.

He didn't look happy, and I suddenly felt the need to defend the woman, especially from Patrick. "But everything ran smoothly. And I think someone on another team asked to speak with her, and the temp didn't turn her away."

Take that, Patrick. He really hated any woman in power.

"That's good, I suppose," Cal said almost to himself. He looked at the eight of us. "Please let me know if you need anything from me. I'm sorry I had to leave for a week right after I just started, but I hope to not have to go back to Chicago for quite some time."

"It's no problem. We understand," someone said.

"Are we going to see you at the Halloween party?" Patrick asked.

Leslie and I exchanged looks and rolled our eyes. Our direct supervisor not only disliked women, but he was also the biggest brownnoser when it came to males in charge. What he didn't understand was that his ass-kissing was so obvious that anyone and everyone knew he wasn't being sincere.

At least, most of us knew. Someone had promoted him to supervisor years ago, but that was before Polly and I had started here. It had been the guy in charge before Polly. I didn't know what had ever happened to him.

Cal smiled. "I plan to be there."

"Are you going to dress up?" Leslie asked. "We have costume contests every year. We have a couples contest and a singles contest, so you'd better bring your A game."

Cal chuckled. "I heard some rumors floating around about that. I have something in mind, but I don't know if it's worth winning a prize. What is the prize usually?"

103

"A hundred dollars out of the manager's pocket," I joked.

Patrick looked horrified and then shot daggers at me.

I ignored him. If he only knew the things I'd done with our boss, Patrick would have a coronary.

Cal threw his head back and laughed. I resisted the urge to shoot Patrick an *I told you so* look.

I looked over to see Leslie holding back what I had to assume was the biggest laugh.

Cal pointed a finger at me. "That's pretty funny. And if you win, I'll give you that hundred bucks."

"She was joking," Patrick said.

Duh, asshole. Cal obviously knows that.

"The real prizes are a dinner for two at a restaurant of their choice for the couples and a fifty-dollar gift card to the store of their choice for the singles costume winner." Patrick smirked. "My wife and I have won the last three years."

As much as I did not like my boss, he and his wife did come up with some cool-ass costumes. Last year, they'd gone as two halves of an avocado, which might not have been that cool, except Patrick's wife had been pregnant so her belly was the pit. Because of that, everyone had voted for them. Even me.

"Ah. Well then, I can't wait to see what you come up with this year."

"We won't disappoint you, sir," Patrick said way too eagerly.

Cal frowned. "It's Cal."

I wanted to laugh, but I didn't. I was sure Cal could see that Patrick was only calling him sir to be a kiss-ass—unlike Keith, who did it on principle. But Keith never kissed anyone's ass. Not even his bosses', which was actually what made him a good assistant. He told it like it was and didn't sugarcoat anything.

Patrick laughed nervously. "Right. Cal. Sorry."

Cal smiled politely. "No need to be sorry. Just a friendly reminder." He turned to the team. "Thanks for the talk, everyone." He looked at me. "Indy, may I have a word with you?"

His tone was serious, and I couldn't deny that I was worried. I had back-talked to my supervisor in a roundabout way when I defended Cal's temp. I hoped I wasn't in trouble.

"Yes, of course."

Cal nodded and headed toward his office.

I shot a quick *uh-oh* look at Leslie and followed him.

Even though Cal and I had slept together, I didn't think I was above getting into trouble. Cal gave the impression that he was a fair and nice boss until you crossed him.

As we reached his office, he held out his arm for me to go inside ahead of him. I didn't say anything as he entered and closed the door behind us. I always cringed in movies or TV when people gave things away because they assumed they knew what the other person was going to say.

No way. Not this gal. I wasn't saying anything until I knew what this impromptu meeting was about.

But then Cal had to leave me hanging by not saying anything. He went around to his desk and sat down. He looked at me, sweeping an arm out to the two chairs sitting in front of his desk. "Sit, please."

I turned my head to take a quick peek out the window to see if anyone was watching, only to realize that the shades were drawn. I hadn't even noticed because I was so nervous as we walked in here.

I took a seat, crossed my legs, and folded my hands in my lap.

Cal leaned back and steepled his fingers by his mouth. "Because of our inclusive…relationship, I feel like I can trust you to tell me the truth without bias. Is this true?"

I wasn't going to lie. "I will try my best to be objective. But if we're being honest, I am only human, and all humans have biases. Even the ones who claim they don't. But I will tell you the truth."

He nodded and dropped his hands. "Understood."

I waited for him to say more, but he almost looked like he was lost in thought.

Finally, he said, "You don't like Patrick Mullen, do you?"

"Uh…"

He lifted an eyebrow. "Remember, you promised to be truthful."

"Okay." I took a deep breath. "No, I don't like him. He's a misogynistic asshole, and how he ever got to be a supervisor, I will never know. I have more knowledge about this job in my one pinkie finger than he does in his whole body."

I'd just had to open my big mouth. I could have said a simple no, but I'd had to go on a rant instead.

"Are you suggesting that you be the supervisor?"

I curled my lip. "God, no. I do not want that responsibility. I like my colleagues, but I do not want to be the one in charge of them."

"Really?"

"Yes." I rolled my eyes. "I always hate those questions on our yearly reviews. *Where do you see yourself in five years?* Why can't I say, *Here, right where I am?* I make good money, it challenges me, but I don't get so stressed out that I need to be on blood pressure meds. Besides, you need people like me to do the work. If we all became supervisors, most of us would have to leave the company because there weren't enough spots to fill." I stopped and took a deep breath.

And if I wasn't mistaken, it looked like Cal was trying not to laugh at me. "You bring up some very good points."

"Thank you, I guess. Does this mean I won't get in trouble when I leave that question blank on my next review?"

"I think it's best you fill it out so that it shows you're a good employee and so there is always a record of that."

"Okay, fine." I'd do it, but I wouldn't like it.

Cal sat forward. "Anyway, going back to Patrick, you said he's a misogynist. Why do you say that?"

"He doesn't like women in charge. He hated Polly even though she was a great boss. And the only reason he complained about the temp is because she was a woman."

Cal nodded, but I wasn't sure if he believed me.

"And then, with you, he kisses your ass."

"Yeah, I noticed that."

"And do you know why?"

"Why?"

"Because you have a penis."

Cal lifted his brow.

"Sorry. My dad is always telling me I'm too much of a feminist. I disagree, but just in case you think the same thing, I wanted you to know that you're not the only one."

"Hmm," he said with the hint of a smile.

"Hmm?" I narrowed my eyes. "Hmm what?"

"You're a feminist, but you don't want to be the boss."

"Cal, I expected better of you."

He looked surprised but also amused.

"Being a feminist is about equality and having choices. I just so happen to *choose* to keep my current position. But if I ever change my mind, I want to know that I could *choose* to move up in the company. Or if I get married and have kids, I could *choose* to be a stay-at-home mom. Or I could *choose* to start my own business."

Cal held up his hand with a smile. "I get it."

"Sorry," I said again.

Cal stood and walked around to my side. He leaned back against his desk. "Someone woke up on the fiery side of the bed today."

I wrinkled my nose. "Huh?"

He laughed. "You're full of fire today."

"I am?"

"You are. Such strong opinions. I like it."

He picked up my hand and drew me into a standing position. He pulled me close, so my breasts were touching his chest.

He took a deep breath as I felt his cock brush my pelvis.

"I do want to talk more about this Patrick situation, but right now, I want to tell you that this outfit is also on fire."

"It is?"

"Oh, yes. This red blouse has been killing me all morning, and all I want to do is take it off you." He slid his hand up my leg. "This too. I can hardly get my work done, thinking about you naked."

"Does this mean you'll fire me if I don't let you?" I joked.

Cal leaned in and sucked on my collarbone. "Never."

"In that case, I think you should do what you've been wanting to do. We wouldn't want your work to suffer."

He kissed up my neck until he reached my mouth. "No, we wouldn't, now would we?"

EIGHTEEN
CAL

"ARE YOU OKAY WITH THIS?" I asked Indy as I slid higher up on the outside of her leg.

"Mmhmm." She wrapped her hands around my neck. "Just don't mess up my hair or my lipstick; otherwise, everyone will know something happened."

I chuckled. "Hair and lipstick. Got it." I squeezed her ass and traced the seam of her panties until I reached the apex of her thighs. "Open."

Indy spread her legs, and I cupped her over her underwear.

"Already wet." I slipped my fingers over the material blocking me from her and pulled until I felt them give with a rip.

She gasped. "What did you do that for?"

"You said, don't mess up your hair or your lipstick. You never said anything about panties."

"I guess I'll have to be more specific next time."

"You do that," I said and pushed two fingers deep inside her.

"Ah, fuck."

"Okay?"

"Better than okay."

I used my other hand to flick open her blouse by a couple of buttons, pulled a bra cup down, and sucked a nipple into my mouth.

She moaned.

I released the hardened bud with a pop. "Shh," I said next to her ear. "People are right outside. They might hear you."

I heard her teeth clamp shut, and she nodded her head.

I pulled her rosebud tip into my mouth again as her pussy coated my hand, and suddenly, I was cursing myself.

I hadn't had sex in almost two weeks. Funny how I had gone months before this, but now, two weeks felt like an eternity.

I should not have started anything with Indy in my office, but my cock had wanted attention and wanted it now. I'd thought I would be able to bring her to orgasm and then go back to work, but it looked like I might have to go into my private bathroom and give my persistent dick some special attention.

I moved on to Indy's other nipple when she reached for my fly. I was about to stop her, but she moved so fast that my cock was in her hand before I could react.

I groaned into her chest as she stroked me. I was going to let myself enjoy her touch for a good twenty seconds, and then I was going to call a halt to this thing.

I straightened, kissing her on the temple. "You need to stop."

"Why? Your body doesn't feel like it wants me to stop."

She emphasized her claim with a squeeze that had me cursing.

"The thing is, if I come, you and I are going to be covered in a mess that's going to be hard to clean up or cover up."

"Hmm…you have a point."

"Unfortunately, I do."

She licked the bottom of my ear. "Do you have a condom?"

I groaned and laughed at the same time. "I can see how you would think that because of the first time we met, but believe it or not, I don't have condoms at work."

"Do you have any diseases I need to worry about?"

I frowned. "No."

Indy managed to turn us around, which wasn't too hard because she had her hand on my dick still, and pushed me onto one of the chairs in front of my desk.

My hand slid from her body as hers did from mine. I wasn't sure which one made me more disappointed.

Indy reached behind herself, and I heard a zipper before her skirt fell off her hips. She caught it with the grace of a woman who'd done this a million times and stepped out of it. "We wouldn't want this to get any more wrinkled than it already is," she said as she laid it out on my desk.

She stood now in a half-buttoned red blouse and a pair of ripped black panties. I reached for her to pull her in between my legs as I yanked what was left of the flimsy material off her. Both sides snapped without much effort, and I snickered as I threw them toward the trash can next to my desk.

I lifted her leg and put it on the back of my chair. "God,

I want to eat you, but I don't trust myself not to smell like you all day." I pressed my fingers into her again, and she moaned. "Fuck it." I shoved my tongue between her legs, making a beeline straight for her clit, as I rubbed her G-spot with my digits.

Pleasuring her like this was the hottest thing I'd ever done at work, but soon, she was swaying on her feet, and I was leaking from my dick. He wanted inside Indy's pussy, like yesterday.

I put her leg down. "Please tell me you're on birth control."

Her eyes were at half-mast, but she managed a nod.

"Thank fuck."

I unbuttoned my dress shirt, yanked my T-shirt up to my chest, and pushed down my dress pants and boxer briefs far enough that they wouldn't get wet from her desire.

I drew her toward me with my hands on her ass. "Come here, sweetheart. It's time for you to get that orgasm I've been teasing out of you."

The chair had no arms, so there was no maneuvering the furniture. It was as if it had been made for fucking.

I slowly lowered her onto my length. Even though I'd been inside her before, she'd never been on top, and we were minus the extra lubrication condoms usually provided.

Although Indy was so wet that no additional help was needed.

I kissed her neck as she slowly took me all the way in. "You feel amazing."

She sighed. "So do you."

She reached the end, and I held her still for a moment. I wanted to enjoy the feeling of just her and me.

"You okay? Am I hurting you?"

"I think if you were any bigger, I'd have turned around and run out of here."

I smiled. "Good thing I'm just right." I encouraged her to move with a nudge to her hips.

Soon, she was clutching my shoulders as she rocked over me.

I cupped her face in my hands. "I want to kiss you so badly."

She smiled. "Same. Stupid work." She kept up the eye contact with me, but then it was like she couldn't any longer. She dropped her forehead to mine, and her legs began to shake.

I wrapped my hand around her dark locks, making sure not to mess it up, and tilted her head back. I peppered a few kisses over her neck and chest before I licked the middle finger of my other hand.

I slipped the wet finger between her cheeks and rubbed her asshole as I bit down on her neck.

A muffled scream erupted from the back of her throat as she bore down on my cock and rode out her orgasm to completion.

My dick was hard as stone and ready to explode. From the moment she'd slid me into her, I had planned to pull her off and come on her stomach. But at the last minute, I changed my mind. I wanted to stay inside of her for as long as possible, and I wanted to know a piece of me would be with her the rest of the day.

I let go of her neck and hair as I held her close, letting her body muffle my moans.

When I felt the room stop spinning and my hearing returned, my office was suddenly silent.

I pulled my head away to look at Indy's face. "Are you okay?"

She grinned at me and nodded. "This is how all Mondays should start."

NINETEEN
CAL

AFTER I HELPED Indy off of me, she went into my private bathroom to clean up and get dressed while I waited in my office.

Not knowing what else to do, I pulled Indy's ripped panties from the floor and used them to clean off my dick, so I could tuck it back in my boxer briefs and pants. I threw her underwear in the empty trash and knew I'd have to do some quick covering up around my office.

Polly, the manager before me, had left her Keurig coffeemaker and a basket full of K-cups. I pulled a cup without even looking at the brand or flavor and put it into the coffeemaker to start it up.

Then, I cleaned out some junk on my desk and top drawer to conceal the item of clothing in my garbage can.

I really hoped my assistant, who missed nothing, wouldn't be able to tell we'd just had sex in my office.

I had moved back to Minnesota without a job, and it had taken me weeks to find one that I wanted. I was either too qualified or not qualified in the right areas. I hadn't even been at my new position a month, and I had just committed a very fireable offense.

I rubbed my hand down my face, frustrated with myself when Indy opened the door.

She appeared like she had when she first stepped into my office. For some reason, that was sexier than if she looked like she'd been rolling around in my bed all night.

"Why are you staring at me like that?" she asked.

I laughed. "Because I can't tell anything happened between us."

She tilted her head in confusion. "Isn't that what we want?"

"Yes, but it makes me want you all over again."

Her eyes widened.

"No one's going to know what went on in here, but I know. And that is fucking hot as hell."

She grinned at me. "Well…" she said, her tone teasing.

"Well what?"

"You might want to take your turn in the bathroom."

Curious as to what she was talking about, I went straight to the mirror.

My hair was still in place, and my shirt only had minor wrinkles. I looked down at my pants but already knew they were in the same state as my shirt.

"Turn your head to the side," she suggested.

I looked to the left. Nothing. I turned to the right. "Oh." Right behind my jaw was a set of dark red lips.

"Sorry."

I smiled at her as I grabbed a paper towel and some soap. "No harm, no foul." I started trying to clean off the mark, and now, half my neck was red, yet you could still pretty much see the lip marks. "What's this stuff made of? Magic marker?"

"It's last-all-day lipstick. It's not supposed to come off, but I put lip balm over it because I hate the dry feeling. It made it wet again." She cringed. "Sorry about that. I do it without even thinking about it." Her eyes brightened, and she held up a finger. "Hold on. Don't rub anymore."

She stepped away, and I heard the mini fridge open. "Yes," she said excitedly. The door closed, and she walked back to the bathroom. "Take off your shirt."

"I think that's what got us into this mess."

She laughed. "Just do it."

"Okay." I yanked the tail of my shirt from my pants and unbuttoned it. I hung it up on the hook behind the bathroom.

"T-shirt too."

I didn't argue, just did as the lady had said. I might know things about business, but I knew nothing about makeup.

Stepping inside the small bathroom with me, she threw away the paper towel from my hand and grabbed a new one.

"Is that half-and-half?" I asked.

She smiled. "Yes. Milk and yogurt can take off lipstick in a pinch, so I figured this was the next best thing."

She poured a little bit onto the towel, holding it over the sink, and wiped it over my neck. I closed my eyes, enjoying the feel of her gentle touch.

"Is it working?" I asked after a few seconds.

"Yes, but it's a slow process. It's not as good as makeup remover."

I kept my eyes closed and let her work. The rhythmic movements were putting me to sleep.

"While we're stuck here, I have another question about Patrick."

She paused for a moment. "Okay." She started cleaning my neck again.

"Has he ever done anything harmful to you?" If he had, I was going to kill him. I'd fire him, and then I'd kill him.

"No. He likes to throw his weight around, and I can tell he doesn't like me or Leslie. The only ones on my team he likes are the guys and Donna—because she is as much of an ass-kisser as he is. But even then, he'll always pick the guys over her if he can."

I frowned. "That's something you should take to HR."

"Pass."

I opened my eyes. "Why would you say that?"

"Because I can't prove anything, and calling up HR with a complaint that is pretty much *he's mean to girls* isn't going to accomplish anything. They might have him take some sensitivity training or some other bullshit, but he'll still be my supervisor. And then he'll make work even harder for me."

I wrapped my fingers around her wrist. "You shouldn't have to work in a toxic environment, Indy."

She smiled sadly and shook her head. "You're so cute."

"Cute? What the fuck does me being cute have to do with this?"

She dropped her hand, and I let go.

"This place isn't the exception, Cal; it's the rule. Women are treated like this in every business everywhere. I'm not saying every man is like this. Not every woman is treated this way, but there is most likely some woman who is being treated like shit by some man—or worse, by men—simply because she's a woman. Unless you're lucky enough to work somewhere that's mostly women, but even then some of the most sexist people I've ever encountered are other women."

I was horrified. "That's awful."

"It's because society teaches us that we're all each other's competition instead of each other's allies." She nodded her head toward me. "Now, tilt your head again, so I can finish."

I closed my eyes once more as she went back to work.

I'd had no idea. My last job had been almost all men, which I could now see was part of the problem that Indy was talking about. I wasn't any better.

"I don't want you to have to work for that asshole anymore."

She didn't respond. I opened my eyes to see her get another paper towel with soap and water. I met her eyes as she drew it over my skin.

She stepped back. "All done."

I pulled her close. "I'm serious, Indy. I'm not going to stand for sexist pieces of shit working here."

She smiled at me, and she actually looked like she was trying not to laugh.

"What's so funny?"

She shook her head. "Nothing. You're just sexy when you're mad."

I wasn't lost on the fact that this was something that men said to women all the time, as if their anger were cute instead of a real feeling that should be validated.

I growled but smiled back. "I'm glad you think I'm sexy."

"I do." She put her hand on my bare chest. "How could

I not with these hot muscles you have hiding under your clothes?"

"I could say the same for you." I looked into the mirror and turned my head. "Hey, you got it."

She smiled at me. "I'm pretty good, aren't I?"

"The best," I said with a grin on my face.

Suddenly, the air felt thick, and awkwardness descended around us. My response was perhaps a little too relationship-like.

She stepped from my arms. "You'd better hurry up and get dressed again, and I should get back out there. People are going to wonder why I was in here for so long."

I hated for her to leave with uncomfortableness between us, but she was right.

I hurried and put both my shirts back on, and then I sat behind my desk as Indy walked out the door.

"Keith," I called out, and my assistant came running.

"My, she was in here a long time."

I could tell Keith had questions about why, but I ignored his comment. "Close the door and sit down, please."

After Keith did as I'd commanded, he asked, "What's going on?"

"I need to find out everything you have on Patrick Mullen."

Keith brightened. "Are you going to finally fire his ass?"

I narrowed my eyes. "You don't like him?"

Keith looked at me like I was stupid. "Are you kidding? He doesn't like anyone who's not white, male, and Christian."

"So, he's not just sexist?"

"He's homophobic and racist, but he'll be the first one to

tell you he likes everyone." Keith rolled his eyes. "It's a fucking joke. Even the other white men in the office steer clear of him."

It was good to know that I had some decent employees out there. But this had me thinking. "Why did Polly put up with him?"

"You don't know?"

"No."

"Patrick's father-in-law is on the board. No one liked him in Chicago, so when this office opened up, he was sent here."

"How do you know all this?"

Keith looked insulted. "Because it's my job to know."

"Right. I mean no offense."

"Well, some was taken," he pointed out.

I held back my smile. I liked my assistant's boldness. "My apologies."

This news meant that it was going to be harder to reprimand someone like Patrick than I had originally thought. I wasn't sure if I wanted to go as far as firing, but I did know he needed to stop treating his employees with bias.

"Keith I need you to schedule some things as soon as possible."

TWENTY
INDY

"WHAT ABOUT A HOT DOG AND A BUN?" I asked Leslie from her couch.

She looked up from her phone from where she sat on the floor. "Uhh…no."

I shrugged. "I don't think it's a bad idea for a costume. It has an underlying sexual joke. He's the hot dog, and you're the bun."

"I am not going as a giant carb. I want to look sexy."

I went back to my phone and continued searching for costume ideas.

"Have you asked Marcus to go yet?"

I smiled guiltily. "No?"

"Was that a question or a statement?"

"Okay, fine. I kind of forgot."

"Indy, it's Saturday. I told you to ask him on Monday."

"I know; I know," I whined. "I got distracted."

"Yeah, by our new boss's penis."

"That's not true." It was kind of true.

We hadn't had sex in the office again all week, but there

had been a couple of stolen touches here and there. And because of this, I didn't feel quite right about asking Marcus to go. Cal and I weren't an item, but I couldn't help but feel like it was cheating. If Marcus asked me, I would probably say yes, but being the initiator made me feel uncomfortable.

"And if you saw his penis, you would be distracted too," I told her.

"Ooh…do tell. You've been kind of secretive about him."

Normally, I told my best friend everything, but it felt wrong to kiss and tell about our boss. I knew Leslie would never do anything, but I didn't want to give anyone any ammo to use against him.

"Sorry, that's all I'm saying."

"Indy, that's not fair. At least tell me how big it is."

I smiled and held my hands up to indicate how long he was.

Leslie gasped. "Shut up. He's that big?"

I lifted a shoulder.

Putting the back of her hand to her forehead, Leslie pretended to faint. "Be still my heart." She snapped back up and narrowed her eyes. "Wait. How thick is it? Because if it's a pencil dick, then who cares how long it is?"

I used both hands to show her Cal's girth because I couldn't do it with one hand.

She put her hand up to her head again. "Be still my vagina."

All I could do was laugh at her.

"What are you going as?" Leslie asked me.

"I have no idea. I've been too worried about your costume."

"I suppose you need to find out if you're taking a date first. If you bring Marcus, you can be a hot dog and a bun."

I wrinkled my nose.

"I saw that," she said, pointing a finger at me. "If you don't want to be a bun, why would I?"

"Point well taken." I scrolled through some more pictures. "What about ketchup and mustard? Chocolate and milk? Peanut butter and jelly?"

"No food. Sexy, remember?"

"Right. Harley Quinn and the Joker?"

"Nah."

I found a picture, and I had to laugh.

Leslie looked up from her phone. "What?"

"You said no food."

"Just tell me."

"If Marcus goes, we could all be a s'more. Two graham crackers, a marshmallow, and a chocolate bar."

"Okay, I kind of like the idea of a group thing, but I still don't like the food theme. And while we'd definitely get everyone's attention, I'm sure people would say we couldn't be in the couples contest because we were a group of four."

"People? Or one person?"

She laughed. "We both know who I'm talking about. He won't give up the prize without a fight."

I lay down on Leslie's couch and stretched out my legs. "What about a favorite TV show or movie? You and Asher could go as a couple on there."

"That's not a bad idea."

"Finally, you like something I suggested," I teased.

"Hey. I said I like the s'mores idea too. In a way."

I snorted. "In a way," I repeated.

I was getting tired of looking at costumes and needed to clear my mind. I put my phone on my chest and closed my eyes.

"Indy?"

I blinked open my eyes. I was on Leslie's couch, and she was standing over me.

"Did I fall asleep?"

"Yeah, for about an hour."

I rubbed my eyes. "Sorry."

"It's okay. That's what Saturdays are for."

I sat up and swung my legs down to the floor. "I can't remember the last time I took a nap. I need to do that more often."

Leslie laughed. "Adult naps are the best." She pointed to the clock on the wall. "Do you want to go and get something to eat? Then, I thought we could come back and watch one of the movies we've been meaning to watch."

I yawned and stretched my arms. "Sounds like a wonderful plan. Even though I just took a nap, I don't feel like doing anything tonight."

"I think it's because we're getting older."

"You shut your mouth."

Leslie laughed and shrugged. "Do you want to pick something up or sit and eat?"

I was wearing leggings and a baggy sweatshirt. Leslie was dressed as comfy as me.

"Let's pick something up. Buca?" I asked.

"I was hoping you'd say that."

Buca di Beppo was one of our favorite restaurants.

We grabbed our purses and left Leslie's place.

Using my phone, I quickly put our order in as Leslie drove. "It should be ready about the time we get there."

"Perfect."

The restaurant wasn't close, but it was one of the best Italian places, so it was a bit of a treat when we picked up food there. When we pulled up, Leslie parked her car and opened her door.

"What are you doing? They bring the food to us."

She danced back and forth. "I have to go to the restroom."

I laughed. "Okay. Hurry back."

She ran into the building, almost knocking over the person coming out. The server walked up to the passenger window and leaned closer.

"Are you Scott?" he asked, referring to the last name on my order.

"Yep."

"Please sign here." He handed me a receipt.

I signed it and handed it back as another vehicle pulled up behind him.

"I'll have your order out here shortly."

"Thank you."

The server walked away, and I glanced into the SUV next to me. The woman in the passenger seat had brown hair. I was about to turn away when I saw the driver stand up and get out of the car.

I gasped and ducked down in my seat. It was Cal, and he was here with another woman.

The awful feeling of jealousy ripped through my chest so quickly that I thought I was going to choke on it.

I hadn't even realized that I liked him that much. But apparently, I did because I wanted to jump out of Leslie's car and punch the other woman in the face. Or at the very least, tell her what we'd done in his office on Monday.

His first day, he had told everyone he wasn't married, but that didn't mean he didn't have a girlfriend. I really didn't want to think he was a cheater. I knew from our conversations that when he'd moved to Minnesota, he was single. So, maybe he had just started dating this woman.

That didn't make me feel much better.

When I heard the footsteps walk away and the door squeaked open, thanks to Leslie's open window, I sat up.

The woman was still sitting in the passenger seat, and she was staring at me like I was a weirdo.

I supposed someone hiding behind the dashboard did look odd.

But in my defense, she was supposed to have gone inside with Cal. Not stay there and watch me look like an ass.

Feeling foolish and not knowing what else to do, I waved at her and said hi.

She waved back but turned away.

I dropped my head back onto the headrest.

I heard the door creak open, and Leslie and the server came outside at the same time. When he realized they were going to the same vehicle, he handed her the food.

"I feel so much better," she said, getting in and handing me the food. "I thought I was going to wet my pants, waiting in line."

"I'm glad."

She looked over at me as she pulled her seat belt on. "You okay?"

"Yeah. Why?"

"You look a little pale."

"Hmm. Must be because I need to eat."

She laughed. "Then, I must look like a ghost because I'm starving."

We got back on the road toward Leslie's house.

"What do you want to watch when we get back?" she asked.

"I don't know. You pick."

"All by myself?" She glanced at me. "Are you sure you're okay?"

"Yep. And I think I am going to ask Marcus to go to the Halloween party."

Leslie grinned. "Woohoo."

I smiled, but I was nowhere near as happy as she was.

TWENTY-ONE
CAL

I CARRIED the tray of tiramisu out the side door of Buca di Beppo and walked up to the passenger door. My sister had the music blaring and couldn't hear me, so I kicked the door.

She jumped, and I laughed at her like any brother would. She turned down the volume.

"Open the door for me."

She got out of the front seat and opened the tailgate in the back. "Why did Mom order so much? That thing's huge."

I set it down and shrugged. "I don't know. Because Dad loves it?"

"They're going to be eating that until the New Year," Amy said, getting back into my SUV.

When we got back to my parents' house, I carried the dessert inside as Amy took my crying nephew from our mother.

"Mom, why did you get so much? You know we're not going to eat all of this in one night," I asked.

My mom pulled the lid off to inspect the tiramisu. "Your father and I are having friends over tomorrow afternoon for his birthday. This way, I only had to put in one order."

"You're so wise."

"Who do you think you got your smarts from, dear?"

I grinned. "You, of course."

"Oh, by the way, your brother's not coming tonight."

"Thank God," I said in a dramatic voice. "You know, Mom, you don't always have to invite the whole family every time I come to dinner."

"*Nicholas Robert Callan.*"

"Yes?" my dad said with a smile as he walked into the kitchen and grabbed a beer from the fridge. My father had been doing this joke since I was little, but for him, it never got old.

"Not you," my mother said. She also always explained to my dad that she was talking to me, as if he didn't know I was the one being reprimanded.

"It's your father's birthday. Of course I'm going to invite my whole family."

"I understand today, Mom. But you know I wouldn't mind coming to dinner and it just being the three of us."

"Then, how are your brother and sister supposed to see you?"

"We live in the same town now."

She stared at me and blinked.

I threw up my hands. "Forget I said anything."

I grabbed my own beer out of the fridge and followed my dad into the living room. Amy was changing the baby on the floor, and her husband, Jon, had their three-year-old in his lap.

"Unca Cal," she said when she saw me and ran over.

I picked her up and took her to the empty recliner to sit. "How's Chelsea?"

"Good," she said with a smile.

"What are you watching?" I asked her since there was a commercial on.

She shrugged. "I don't know. Grandpa's show."

"What are you watching, Dad?"

"Some movie."

I rolled my eyes. My dad never knew the name of anything.

"It's *Transformers*," Jon said.

"Dad, how could you not know it's *Transformers*? They literally transform."

My dad's response was to grunt.

Amy looked at her husband. "Is this appropriate for Chelsea to watch?"

"She's fine. It's PG-13."

"And she's only three." My sister got up from the floor and handed her husband the baby. "Come on, Chelsea. Let's go help Grandma."

Chelsea laid her head on my chest. "I want to stay with Unca Cal."

"Fine." She sighed. "I'll go help Grandma."

After my sister left, I thought about what Indy had said on Monday about sexism. And the fact that my mom and sister were in the kitchen, making dinner, while us guys were out in the living room, watching TV.

I lifted Chelsea off my lap and set her on the floor. "I'm going to go help your grandma, kiddo. Why don't you go back and sit with your dad?"

I stood, and she grabbed my hand.

"I go wiff."

I led my niece back into the kitchen, and my mom glanced up at me before turning back to the food she was preparing.

"Need another beer, Cal?"

"Nope. Chelsea and I came to help."

My mom and sister both looked up at me at the same time and the same way. I laughed at how much alike they were.

"Did I just hear that right?" Amy asked.

"Yes." I picked up Chelsea and set her on one of the kitchen stools, so she could see. "What can we do?"

Mom grabbed a large bowl, a hand mixer, and a box of cake mix in front of Chelsea and me. "You can make the cake."

"Cake and tiramisu?"

"Not everyone likes tiramisu."

"I yike cake," Chelsea said.

"See," my mom pointed out.

I smiled. "I see."

My niece and I—more me than my niece—went to work on the cake.

"How's work?" my sister asked me.

"It's good. I like it. Different from what I did in New York, but not so different that I feel completely lost."

"That's good."

After a few seconds, I asked, "Can I ask you two a question?"

"What's wrong, dear?" Mom said.

"Nothing's wrong. I'm just wondering if you've ever experienced sexism on the job."

Mom and Amy exchanged looks.

"What?" I asked them.

My mom turned around. "Did something happen? Was there a complaint filed?"

"Wait. You think I'm the one being sexist?" I waved my hands in front of my face. "No, no, no. It's not me. It's one of my employees."

Mom put her hand on her chest in relief. "Oh, thank God. I didn't raise my sons to treat women badly."

I scowled. "I'm a little offended that you would think that about me."

"Cal, it's not like Mom and I think you would do something like that on purpose. Even decent guys can be sexist and not know it."

"That doesn't seem like a good excuse," I said.

Amy looked surprised. "That's great to hear you say."

"What are you going to do about your employee, Cal?" Mom asked. "And I'm sorry if I hurt your feelings. I apologize for jumping to conclusions."

"Thanks, Mom. And I thought I would start with sensitivity training."

Amy scoffed. "You know everyone's going to hate it and make fun of it behind your back."

I shrugged. "Yeah, probably. But I have to start somewhere. I want to make sure HR says I did everything I could before I get rid of this guy."

My mom walked over to me and squeezed my face, pulling me down to kiss me on the forehead. "Whatever you do, I know you'll do the right thing."

"That's not the way you felt two minutes ago," I said through fish lips since she still had her hand cupping my face.

Chelsea laughed. "Unca Cal looks funny."

Mom let me go, and I rubbed my cheeks.

"That's because Uncle Cal is funny," she told Chelsea.

"Mom's right, Cal. I'm proud of you for not ignoring this," Amy said, and I could see the pride in my little sister's eyes.

"Thanks. I'm going to do my best."

TWENTY-TWO

INDY

MONDAY MORNING HUNG over my head like a dark cloud. I didn't want to go to work for several reasons. I didn't want to see Cal and face the fact that I might have feelings for him. I didn't want to expend the energy I knew it was going to take to avoid him. And I didn't want to start the stupid sensitivity training that was supposed to last all week.

I really did appreciate Cal's efforts to improve things, but when it came to guys like Patrick, they weren't going to change. Mostly because they didn't know there was anything wrong with the way they viewed the world.

"Hey, Indy," Leslie said as she got to her desk that morning.

"Hey."

She pulled out her chair and sat down. "You look bummed."

"I'm just not looking forward to this week."

"Oh, yeah. The extra training classes."

"Exactly."

Leslie shrugged. "I don't mind. If we get paid to sit there, I'm not going to complain. I heard the company that conducts the training actually tries to make things more interesting."

"That's what I'm worried about. What if we have to act out scenarios? I always feel so stupid, getting up in front of everyone." I leaned toward her. "And since we're doing this in teams, that means we have to put up with Patrick the whole time."

Leslie frowned and cocked her head. "I thought all the supervisors were doing a class together."

This was good news. "They are?"

"That's what I thought the email said."

I quickly pulled up my work email and reread the message from last week. Leslie was right. "Well, I'll be. I wonder why they're doing it that way."

"So that we're with our peers." She shrugged. "That's my guess." Leslie looked around and leaned toward me this time. "I also heard that while the supervisors are going to have this meeting, Cal is going to pull us all aside and talk about how we need to file complaints to make management and HR aware of sensitive situations."

"Wow. I had no idea." I frowned. "How do you know this?"

"Keith told me." She studied my face. "I'm surprised you didn't know. Didn't Cal tell you?"

There were a lot of things I was surprised I didn't know about Cal. This was just one of them. "No, but I didn't talk to him this weekend much."

Friday, we had both been busy, and Saturday, he'd texted me later that night, but I didn't answer. Not after seeing him with someone else. I sent him a quick message yesterday morning, telling him I had already been asleep and left it at that. Then, I'd pretended to be busy the rest of the day.

"Do you think he'll call you into his office again like he did last Monday?"

God, I hope not. It would be really hard to keep my hands off of him if we were alone together.

I shrugged. "I don't know, but I would guess no. He's going to have his hands full with the extra training this week."

Leslie smiled. "I'm sure he'll find a way to speak to you if he really wants to."

I didn't know if Leslie was right or if I was just unlucky.

First thing that morning, I ran into Cal as I was going into the restroom and he was coming out. We were the only two in the hall, so I couldn't pretend like I was an average employee.

He smiled when he saw me. "Hey, Indy."

I smiled back and hoped he couldn't tell my heart wasn't in it. "Hi, Cal."

"How was your weekend?"

"Good. And yours?"

I held my breath, waiting for him to say something to make me stop obsessing over what I had seen on Saturday.

He lifted a shoulder. "It was pretty boring."

I felt my heart constrict. I didn't know if boring meant

he hadn't had fun with this other woman or if he was simply saying it as a way to not mention her.

But then he stepped closer, and my body melted as he touched my hip.

My body was not on board with how my brain had decided to take a step back to protect myself.

"I'd rather have spent it with you," he said in my ear.

Now, why did he have to go and say that?

He ran his nose down my neck. "It's been a whole week since I've been inside you, and it's killing me."

Damn him.

I turned my head and kissed him.

His tongue thrust into my mouth, and I groaned at the taste of him. I grabbed on to his sides and squeezed. I wanted him closer. I wanted him naked.

The sound of laughter broke through my sexual haze, and I ripped my mouth away.

Cal rested his head on my forehead, breathing hard, but I stepped to the side.

He frowned. "You okay?"

"Yeah. I'm just worried someone will find us."

He took a deep breath. "Yeah, you're right. I probably shouldn't be caught kissing an employee when everyone's going to be learning about harassment this week."

Despite my heavy heart, I had to smile at the hypocrisy.

"You'd never fire me or give me a bad review if I told you no more sex, would you?"

His eyes narrowed. "Hell no."

He said it so loud and with such conviction that I looked behind me to make sure no one was coming.

I turned back to Cal and patted him on the shoulder.

"See, you're not a sexual harasser." I walked around him and headed into the women's room.

I walked up to the mirror and cursed myself. Why I'd felt the need to make him feel better irked me. I should have let him stew in his own guilt.

And I shouldn't have kissed him. Thank God I was wearing lip gloss instead of my all-day lipstick today. I grabbed some toilet paper from a stall and fixed my lips.

I needed to stay away from that man.

On Tuesday, my team and another team were scheduled for training. We were all crammed into the conference room where at least I didn't have to see Cal all day. The information was good, but it was all stuff that I'd already known, as had most people. And Leslie was right because I could totally see Patrick thinking the whole thing was bullshit and a waste of time.

On Wednesday, I had no run-ins with Cal either, and work felt a little more like normal.

"I think I finally know what Asher and I are going to the party as," Leslie announced that morning.

"So soon?" I teased. "You still have three days until the party."

She flipped her hair over her shoulder. "I'm choosing to ignore your negativity because I am excited."

"Spill it. Who are you going as?"

"Aquaman and Mera."

"Okay"—I held up my hands—"you two are going to be so hot."

Leslie squeaked. "I know." She ran her hands down the sides of her body. "My outfit is tight, and it's going to show off my bod. And the girls get to be on display." She pretended to pick up her boobs.

I laughed. "And is Asher going to wear the outfit, or is he going to wear jeans and no shirt like in the beginning of the movie?"

"Oh, he's wearing the outfit. I don't need everyone drooling over my man."

"That's probably a wise decision."

"Are you and Marcus still going as a nurse and patient?"

Leslie wasn't impressed with our costume idea, but I liked it. I was going as a sexy nurse because I could fully admit I wanted to make Cal drool. And Marcus was going as my patient because I didn't want him to spend any money. I felt bad about taking him as my date when my heart wasn't all the way into it, but that was what happened when I asked someone out on a date when I was upset.

"Yes," I told her. "Marcus already has crutches from when he broke his leg in college. And we're going to wrap his leg in an ACE bandage. It will be fine. I'm not trying to win the prize like you are." I didn't want to be stuck going on another date if I didn't like this one.

"Whatever you say. I still think you could do better."

On Thursday, Cal pulled our whole team into his office and went over the things we'd learned. He stressed that we needed to take action if we wanted things to change. We all kind of exchanged looks, but I doubted that anyone was going to write Patrick up. He'd never actually said outright sexist things. It would be difficult to prove that he didn't pick women for certain projects when the men were just as capable.

I thought Cal realized that his efforts were failing. He

looked dejected as he talked to us, and he couldn't seem to muster up much encouragement. I felt bad for the guy.

So, when everyone else stepped out, I stayed behind. "Cal?"

He looked up from his desk but didn't smile when he saw it was me. "Yeah?"

"I know you want to make this place better, but sometimes, things just are what they are. I don't think anyone is going to do anything about Patrick because the guy knows right where to draw the line."

Cal didn't say anything. He simply stared at me with an almost-blank look, and I started to wonder if he was mad that I had said something.

"I'm sorry. You just look so sad——"

"I'm not sad. I'm pissed."

I took a step back, not expecting the anger to roll off him like it did.

His look changed to irritation. "Just go, Indy."

"Are you sure there's nothing——"

"Go," he snapped, and I jumped. He closed his eyes and opened them, meeting my gaze. "I'm sorry. It's been a long week."

I nodded and backed up toward the door. I didn't know where I got the balls to speak again, but I asked, "Are you still coming to the party on Saturday?"

Cal took a deep breath. "I don't know at this point."

I thought about telling him that I really wanted to see him there, but I didn't want to give him the wrong idea. "There will be alcohol at the party. You could get Patrick drunk and buddy up to him. He might show his true colors away from work." I smiled reassuringly. "Just think about it."

I headed to the door and walked out.

Cal didn't come out of his office all day on Friday, and he hadn't texted since the weekend.

I was beginning to think I didn't need to avoid him anymore.

TWENTY-THREE
CAL

I ALMOST STAYED HOME Saturday night, but several things convinced me to go. I was still new at my job, and I didn't want my employees to think I had better things to do than hang out with them. I had also considered Indy's advice about Patrick. I could either ask him out for drinks or take the opportunity that was presented to me and pretend to befriend him. I couldn't pass it up because I had no desire to ask Patrick to get drinks with me after work and spend any more time with him than I had to.

The biggest reason I wanted to go was that Indy had been avoiding me all week. I hadn't pressured her or tried to get her alone after she walked away from me on Monday because I wasn't going to be that guy. That would put me in line with Patrick.

But I was hoping to at least sit down and talk to her. Ask her what had happened and why things had changed. I liked Indy. I liked being with her—not just sexually—and I didn't want to give her up without a fight.

I showed up early, fully expecting to be one of the first

ones at the party. The employees in charge of putting the event together had rented a ballroom at a local event center, which was now covered in Halloween decor.

There was a cash bar, a table covered in food, tables and chairs, a DJ booth, and a dance floor. When my employees had talked about a costume contest, I should have guessed that they went all out for the event, but I was surprised.

I was also shocked at how many people were already there. I guessed there was no such thing as fashionably late for this group of people.

"Hi, Cal." One of my older employees waved to me. "Nice costume."

I waved back but didn't stop to chat. I needed a drink first.

As I waited for the bartender to grab my beer, I looked around for Patrick. It was going to be harder to find him with everyone dressed up, but since I remembered that he and his wife had won the costume contest before, I ruled out any badly dressed people as Patrick.

I should have dressed in something with a mask, so people wouldn't recognize me right away, and then I could have blended in better. Instead, I had decided to dress as a doctor. I'd already had the scrubs, surgical cap, and stethoscope from when I'd worn the getup one year in New York. I figured a new location was a good excuse to recycle an old costume.

The bartender handed me my bottle when I thought I spotted Patrick. He was dressed as a 1920s gangster, and the woman who I assumed was his wife had on a flapper outfit.

I didn't think it was the most original couples costume, but I could see they had gone all out and put a lot of details into their outfits. Maybe that was why Patrick won every year. All that stuff cost money that most people didn't want to waste on one night.

I was about to head over to Patrick when I saw Leslie—or at least, it looked like Leslie but with red hair—walk in. She had a very tall man with her, dressed as Aquaman, and I then recognized her as the water heroine in the movie. I couldn't remember the name of the character, and I made a mental note to look it up on my phone before I went over to talk to her.

Leslie and Aquaman turned once they were inside the room, and I realized that they were probably waiting for Indy.

I held my breath as I stopped and waited too.

Indy walked in, wearing the naughtiest nurse costume I'd ever seen. I wasn't sure it was even low enough to cover her ass. My dick got hard as she laughed at something.

Wanting to know what had made her smile like that, I tore my eyes away from her to the doorway. A guy came in on crutches with a bandaged foot. He wobbled as he tried to use them and dropped down to both feet.

Indy, Leslie, and Aquaman all laughed at him, and the guy smiled and shrugged. He held the crutches out to Indy, and she shook her head and waved her hands back and forth. He stepped closer with ease—his foot was obviously fine—and put the crutches in her hands. The tops of them were over her shoulders. But rather than adjust them, she handed them back.

The guy put an arm around Indy and hugged her.

I didn't like it one bit.

The guy looked closer to her age than mine and was

handsome. And if I had to guess, he was her date. It pissed me off. If this was the reason she'd been avoiding me all week, she could have just told me. We weren't children, and I could have handled the news.

I wanted to march over there, pull her aside, and ask her what kind of game she was playing, but I ignored my baser instincts. I was nearing forty, and I was too tired for mind games anymore.

I headed over to Patrick—my original target.

"Hello, Patrick."

He spun around and grinned. "Hello. You came."

I took a long drink of my beer. "I couldn't disappoint the employees," I joked.

Patrick laughed at my bad joke and pulled the lady next to him forward. "Cal, this is my wife, Jeanie."

She held out her hand, and I shook it.

"Hello, Jeanie. I'm Cal."

She smiled at me. "I've heard a lot about you."

"Thank you. You two look like you went all out on your costumes tonight."

Patrick even had a fake Tommy gun.

"I hope that thing's not real."

Patrick laughed again and shook it back and forth. "You never know."

I wished it were real. Tommy guns were illegal. If he were arrested on a firearms charge, I wouldn't have to worry about getting rid of him.

"Can I get you a drink?" I asked.

"You don't need to do that." He slapped Jeanie on the ass. "The old wife will get one for me, won't you?"

"Of course, dear."

Jeanie took off for the cash bar, and I searched my brain for something to say to Patrick.

"It figures Leslie would be dating someone like that."

I looked up from my beer. "What? I'm sorry. I missed that."

Patrick pointed to Leslie and Aquaman. "It figures she'd be dating someone like that. I always took her for...the *adventurous* type."

I wasn't sure what he meant by that, but his tone of voice told me it wasn't something I would like.

I took a drink and acted dim. "Oh? I guess I don't know since I haven't worked with her much."

"Leslie *dates* a lot," Patrick said. He nudged me in the arm. "If you get my meaning."

Yeah, I got it. When he said *adventurous*, he meant slutty. *What a dick.*

"You don't say." I shrugged. "I guess what people do in their own time is up to them. As long as they get their work done and do a good job, I'm not going to judge."

"Oh, oh, me either," Patrick was quick to reply.

Bullshit.

Patrick leaned closer. "It's just...she doesn't look like she makes the best choices."

I looked Patrick in the eye. "You mean, because her boyfriend's black?"

He tried to look offended, but it was all fake. "I would never think that about anyone. I was merely pointing out the fact that he's tall and muscular."

What his height and body shape had to do with best choices, I didn't know, but I decided not to ask. If I spent more time with Patrick, I'd have to go and take a shower.

Plus, he was smart enough to not say anything more offensive out loud. Any lawyer could argue that he meant something else.

"I'd better go make the rounds," I said and walked away. "Tell your wife bye." *And give her my sympathies.*

Wanting to get away, I didn't pay much attention to what was in front of me until I ran into someone.

TWENTY-FOUR

INDY

I LOOKED up to see Cal standing over me. Even though I had heels on, he was taller than me.

He was dressed as a doctor, and he made scrubs look good. It was just my luck that his costume went with mine better than my own date's.

I hate you, universe.

"Hey," I said lamely.

"Hi." His jaw was clenched tight.

"Everything okay?"

"Hey, you two are dressed as a doctor and a nurse," someone said, walking by us.

I crossed my arms over my chest and laughed uncomfortably. "Maybe we should have discussed our costumes before we came tonight," I joked.

"Yeah, maybe. But in order to have a discussion, two people need to be speaking to one another." His words were sharp, and I knew that he knew I'd been avoiding him.

I dropped my hands to my sides. "I'm sorry, Cal."

"If you'll excuse me, it looks like someone is trying to get my attention." He looked behind me, and I turned to look. "Why don't you go back to your date?"

I gasped and swung back around, but he was already gone.

Leslie skipped up to me while my mouth was still hanging open.

"What happened?"

I told her the exchange I'd just had with Cal.

"Oh my God, he's jealous." She clapped her hands. "He's jealous because he likes you."

I shook my head. "I don't think so. He's probably just mad because I've been blowing him off."

"He's mad because you've been blowing him?" She put her hand to her ear. "I'm sorry, I didn't catch that."

I laughed and playfully shoved her. "Shut up."

"Kidding. Kidding. He might be mad that you're blowing him off. But that's because he likes you."

I rolled my eyes. "No, he doesn't."

Leslie frowned. "Why are you fighting this so hard?"

Because I liked him, and I didn't want to get my hopes up that he liked me. Because there was no way he could like me and go on a date with someone else.

But I still hadn't told Leslie what I'd seen last weekend. It made me feel like a fool. And while my friend loved me dearly and would never think badly of me, I was still too embarrassed. I wanted to just forget it had ever happened.

"Let's not argue about some guy," I told her. "We're here to have fun tonight."

She smiled. "You're right." She put her arm in mine. "Come with me, so I can put my and Asher's names down for the couples contest."

"Lead the way."

We walked over to the contest table. Everyone who wanted to enter had to put their names down. At some point in the night, the list would be cut off from anyone else entering, and that was when people would be allowed to vote. There were two clipboards—one for singles and one for couples—and two black boxes. Right now, they were covered, so no one could sneak extra votes into them.

Our work took this very seriously.

Leslie picked up the couples clipboard. "Are you sure you don't want me to put your name down?"

"Yes, I'm positive."

"What about the singles contest?"

"Nope. I'm all good."

I wasn't in the mood to compete with anyone tonight.

Leslie scribbled away and set the clipboard back down. She had a cunning smile on her face, and I knew she was up to something. I turned to look but was yanked away as she grabbed my hand.

"Let's go dance." She pulled me behind her until we reached the edge of the dance floor.

I put my hands on my hips. "What did you do?"

She looked at me, confused. "What do you mean?"

"Back there. You looked like the cat who ate the canary. Did you cross off Patrick's and his wife's names?"

She looked genuinely surprised by my question. "No." She shook her head. "I wouldn't do that. If—no, when—Asher and I win, it's going to be because we played fair and beat last year's winners. No cheating."

She seemed sincere, so I believed her.

"I think you've got this in the bag. You and Asher look way better than Patrick and Jeanie."

She smiled. "We do, don't we?"

"Don't get a big head now. No one will vote for you then."

She laughed. "I won't get a big head if you dance with me."

I couldn't help but smile. "Deal."

A new song started less than a minute later, and we walked out to join the small crowd already dancing. It was harder to dance in front of your coworkers than strangers, and it occurred to me that I should get a drink.

I was about to tell Leslie that I would go to the bar for the both of us when Asher and Marcus came dancing up, all four hands full.

Marcus handed me a glass.

"How did you know what I wanted?" I asked in his ear.

"It's what you ordered the night we went to the club. I hope it's okay."

I took a long drink. "It's perfect." I looked around. "Where are your crutches?"

"I left them at a table. I thought it might be easier to dance without them."

"Good call." I drank the rest of my alcohol and set my glass down at the nearest table.

I came back to Marcus and wrapped my arms around his neck. He held a beer in his one hand, but the other went around my waist as he pulled me close. I smiled up at him.

I was glad I had asked him to come. I couldn't see myself ever getting romantically involved with him, but I liked hanging out with him. He had made us all laugh as he attempted to use his crutches to get into the building. I had to give him credit for trying to stay in costume.

We danced for a few more songs, and I was beginning to get overheated.

"After this song, I'm going to go and get a drink."

Fingers wrapped around my upper arm. "Why don't you go and get that drink now?" Cal said.

Marcus frowned at Cal's hand on me.

Cal dropped his arm. "We need to talk."

"You okay?" Marcus asked, and Cal narrowed his eyes at my date.

I rolled my eyes. "He's my boss. I'm fine." I put my hand on Marcus's chest even though warning sounds went off in my head. "You stay and dance or get some food. I'll come and find you."

Marcus nodded, but I could tell he was still worried.

"I'll be fine. I promise."

I didn't look at Cal as I walked off the dance floor. I could feel him right behind me.

When we were a good distance away, I turned to Cal and crossed my arms over my chest. "Where do you want to talk?"

TWENTY-FIVE

CAL

"OUT IN THE HALL," I told Indy.

She huffed out a breath and headed for the double doors that led to the hallway.

Once outside the ballroom, it was quieter and brighter. Indy's cheeks were flushed from dancing with her date, and jealousy raged through my body.

I looked away from her before I grabbed her and kissed her where anyone could see us. As my eyes wandered the hall, I noticed a room marked for storage and pointed. "In there?"

She wrinkled her nose and crossed her arms again.

I really wished she'd stop doing that. It pushed her already-revealed breasts up even further. I was worried her nipples were going to pop out.

And I didn't want anyone seeing them but me. Especially that guy she'd brought with her tonight.

"Cal."

"What?"

She moved her hands to her hips. "You didn't even hear me."

I grabbed one of her hands and pulled her toward the storage room. "What did you say?"

"I said, we're not going in there."

I opened the door and pushed her in before closing it. "Too late."

"I can't see anything."

"You don't need to see anything." I backed her up against the wall. I held a hand out to make sure she didn't bump her head or anything. But rather than run into any shelves, we ran into a counter. "Perfect."

"What's perfect?" she asked suspiciously.

I put a hand on her hip and quickly ran it up her side and around to her front. I found the zipper that held her naughty nurse outfit together and jerked it down.

She inhaled sharply as I picked her up and set her ass on the counter.

"What are you doing?" she hissed.

"Taking what's mine."

I cupped the back of her neck and tilted her head the way I wanted, so I could kiss her like I'd been dying to do all night.

She fought for two seconds before she moaned and opened her mouth for me. Her hands came up, and she fisted the front of my shirt. I was ready for her to push me away, but I mentally cheered when she pulled me closer.

The fact that she was so wild for me made me hotter. I wanted to take my time with her and taste her all over, but I knew we both couldn't be gone forever before people started to notice. We had left the ballroom together.

I grabbed for the sides of her panties and pulled my mouth away. "I'm sorry to do this again," I said.

"Do what?" she asked breathlessly.

I snapped both sides of her underwear, breaking the thin material, and she gasped.

"You're an asshole," she said.

I yanked her ass to the edge. "I guess, tonight, I am." I found the string holding my scrub pants and yanked.

"Why?"

I pulled her legs up over my hips and shoved inside her. I hadn't even checked to see if she was ready. I dropped my forehead on hers. "Goddamn it. It's like you bring out the barbaric side in me."

I really was an asshole, but I sent a silent thank-you out in the world that she had already been wet for me.

"Are you going to stand there all day, or are you going to fuck me?"

A grin split over my face, and I gradually withdrew from her body and then gently pushed back in.

Indy's moan was music to my ears.

I slowly thrust into her a few more times before increasing my pace. I knew I could bring her to orgasm with just my cock, but I wanted to make her come now.

I pulled out and shoved my thumb in her pussy. The best lubricant was the natural female one if it was available. I dragged my thumb up to her clit and entered her again as I swirled my digit around her swollen nub.

"Fuck me," she cried out.

"I am, baby. I already am."

Her fingers were digging into my back. "Please don't stop. If you stop, I'll kill you."

"Don't worry. I've got you."

I bent my knees and angled my cock upward for a few strokes, and Indy's climax came barreling upon her like a car going a hundred miles per hour. Her whole body shook, and her vagina clenched down around my dick.

I let her ride the wave for a good thirty seconds before I began to thrust again.

She tried to swat at my hand. "I'm done."

I kissed her and flicked her clit. "You're not done yet."

She whimpered, "I can't."

"Yes, you can."

The second time, it took me a little longer to make her come, but her orgasm was just as satisfying for me. I hoped it was for her too.

I would have loved to stay there all night, making her climax over and over, but my own body was tired of waiting. And like I said, we were pressed for time.

Using both hands, I cupped her ass and brought her as flush to me as I could before I exploded, emptying myself inside of her.

All too soon, I withdrew from her body and pulled up my pants. I tried to find a light switch on the wall but didn't have any luck, so I took my phone from my pocket and turned on the flashlight.

Indy jumped off the counter and looked down her legs as what was left of her underwear fell to the floor.

With a deep breath, she zipped up her dress while I picked up her panties.

"Look, if we're going to be having sex with other people, we can't be having sex without condoms."

Her words had me standing up awfully fast.

"What are you talking about?" Her date crossed my mind, but I replayed her tone in my head. Her words had been accusatory, not informative. "Is this why you've been avoiding me?"

She shrugged and lifted her chin. "We never talked about being exclusive, so I think it's wise that we always practice safe sex."

I laughed, which she didn't seem to like by the scowl on her face. "Honey, you're the only person I've been with in months. Months," I repeated the word, so it would penetrate her brain.

She didn't look convinced, so I stepped closer, making her take a step back until she hit the counter she'd just been sitting on.

"In fact, when I was in New York, my old girlfriend came to my goodbye party. She was ready to give me a great send-off, if you know what I mean. And when I say old girlfriend, I mean, someone I dated for over four years."

"So, what happened? She came to her senses?"

I put my hands on Indy's hips and kissed her neck. "No, because we both know I'm good in bed."

She snorted, but I felt her fingers sneak up my shirt and touch my bare stomach.

"I really didn't want to be with her, but when she tried to corner me and kiss me, all I could think about was you."

She stiffened. "I don't believe you."

I shrugged and kissed her smooth skin again. "Believe me. Don't believe me. It's the truth though."

She took a deep breath and relaxed a little. "So, where does this leave us?"

I looked up at her. It was hard to see her face since the

hand holding the phone was also on her hip, pointing the light to the floor.

I moved the flashlight, so we could see each other better. "Where do you want this to leave us?"

She shook her head. "I asked you first."

She looked strong and confident, standing in front of me in nothing but a short dress and my cum on her thighs, but for a second, I saw a glimmer of vulnerability in her eyes.

"This means"—I reached between her legs and coated my fingers with my seed before bringing my hand up and running my finger over the upper swell of her right breast—"that you"—I ran my other finger over her left breast—"are mine."

She stared down at her chest with her mouth open. "What was that for?"

"So, your little date out there smells me on you and stays away."

She looked up at me and narrowed her eyes. "Alpha males suck."

She stomped past me toward the door, but I grabbed her hand and yanked her back to me.

"*Oof.*"

I smiled down at her. "This means, I don't want to sleep with anyone else, Indy." I gave her a serious look. "But this also means you don't sleep with anyone else either."

"I suppose I can do that."

I laughed at her stubbornness and kissed her. "I also want you to come home with me tonight."

TWENTY-SIX

INDY

I SHOOK MY HEAD. "I can't."

Cal frowned.

"At least, not right away," I added. "We all rode together. But once Leslie and Asher drop me off at home, I can come over." Although I wanted to go home with Cal right now—screw the rest of the party—I needed to pack some clothes. I was not going to wear a nurse's uniform home tomorrow from his house.

"Okay, I guess that works."

I studied his face in the dim light. "Are you sure you want to be exclusive?"

"The fact that you even have to ask means I'm doing something wrong."

I put my hands on his chest. "Not wrong. It's just work and *you being my boss* sort of thing."

"I'll do some digging with HR on the rules, and until then, it will be our little secret."

I nodded in agreement. "That's smart. Even if our relationship is allowed, you just started. I don't want anyone thinking anything about you other than you're a good boss. And I don't want them to think you're going to play favorites with me. If we show them that you treat me like everyone else for a while, then they can't complain."

"Does this mean, no Monday office sex?" he asked.

I laughed and kissed him.

He wrapped his arms around me and deepened the kiss.

I forced myself to pull away. "Going by that reaction, I think we're going to have to be careful with what we do around the office. Including how much time I spend in your actual office."

"So smart and so sexy."

I couldn't help it; his compliment went straight to my heart.

"Speaking of time, we'd better get back in there."

"Yeah. I should probably use the restroom first."

Cal growled. "No way. The only thing that will keep me sane while you go and finish your date is knowing a part of me is inside you."

His words had my belly doing a flip and my pussy clenching. I ran a finger down his nose. "Alpha male."

"Why do you keep saying that?"

"Never mind," I said with a smile. "Let's get back out there."

Cal snorted and pushed me back until we reached the door. "I'll go first." He kissed my temple, opened the door, and peeked around. "Coast is clear. See you back in there."

I watched him go, counted to a hundred and twenty, and followed. Of course, I stopped at the restroom to do a quick clean job first. As much as his possessive streak turned me on, I wasn't going back out there, covered in his cum.

I managed to slip back into the ballroom without anyone noticing. I walked around the outside so that I didn't have to mingle. Plus, that way, when someone asked, I could say I'd been around; they just hadn't noticed.

I went to the cash bar and ordered a drink. I had shoved money in one of the two tiny pockets on my outfit before I left home, and thankfully, it was still there. I sipped on my drink and made conversation with one of my coworker's wives, who was standing by herself.

When the DJ made the announcement that all the entries for the costume contests needed to be in, I excused myself and went to find my friends.

When I approached, they all looked at me, and I fought to act cool.

"Marcus said that Cal pulled you away to talk."

I waved off Leslie's concern. "Oh, yeah, that was some time ago. I've been over there, talking to Ed's wife." I pointed to where Ed's wife was standing.

Leslie almost looked disappointed. She leaned in closer to me. "I want all the details later. Every. Last. One."

I ignored her and smiled apologetically at Marcus. "I'm sorry. I've been a bad date."

He smiled. "It's okay. I've been hanging out with these two."

"Chicken," she whispered in my ear.

I tilted my head and smiled at her. "Careful, or I'm giving my vote to Patrick."

She gasped. "You wouldn't."

I batted my eyelashes at her.

"Fine. I love you, and I will never bother you again."

"Yes, you will. But I love you too."

The coworkers who had put the party together started walking around, handing out paper and pens.

I knew the drill from years past, but the DJ still announced, "Everyone is getting two pieces of paper. Please write down your choices for the winners and get in line. If you don't know who has entered, you may wait to put a name down when you get to the front."

Despite my teasing, I put down Leslie's and Asher's names for the couple and got in line. The clipboards were hanging on a pole toward the front of the line, and I noticed some people were pointing out someone on the list and looking around. A lot of eyes fell on Cal, and I wondered if he had entered.

He didn't really seem like the kind of person who would want to be in a contest, much less win over his employees, and my curiosity grew.

A few people even turned around and glanced back at me and my friends. I assumed they were checking out Leslie's and Asher's costumes.

We were almost to the clipboards, and Leslie was staring off to the distance, so I figured now was the time to share some of my secret naughty times.

I leaned close to her ear. "I'm not wearing any underwear because Cal broke them."

She gasped, and her eyes lit up. "You slut," she said with a smile.

I grinned back at her.

"Tell me more."

"Sorry. It's our turn." I stepped forward and scanned the singles costume list. Cal wasn't on it. I didn't have time to dwell that detail, so I quickly picked someone and wrote their name down.

When the four of us were done voting, we went and sat down. I knew it would take some time to count the votes, so I went to grab some food to eat. Having sex in a storage room at a work party sure brought out the appetite in me.

When I got back, Leslie was smiling at me like she had done something sneaky, and I narrowed my eyes.

"Why are you acting suspicious?" I asked.

She held up her hands. "I don't know what you're talking about."

I popped a chip in my mouth. "Yeah, right."

"Hey, Indy?" Asher said.

"What?"

"We talked about going out after this and getting some more mileage out of our costumes. You in?"

I looked guiltily at Marcus. He'd really wasted his Saturday night, coming to this work party with me, for which I hadn't even hung out with him for half the time. And now, I was going to ditch him to go to another guy's house.

"I think I'm going to go home," I told the table. I looked at Marcus. "I'm sorry."

"Don't be sorry."

"I can't help it. You're probably bored."

He laughed and shook his head. "Really, it's fine."

I leaned toward him. "Just in case I forget to tell you, Veronica is a fool."

He smiled shyly. "Actually, the two of us have been talking for the last couple of days."

"And you still came here tonight? You didn't have to."

"No, that wouldn't have been right for me to bail on you. Besides, it's good Veronica knows that I'm not sitting around, waiting for her."

I held up my fist, and he bumped it.

"That's right, Marcus. You show her you're worth it."

The music was turned down as the DJ stepped up to the mike.

Leslie clapped her hands. "It's time for the results." She peered over at Patrick and his wife. "Those two are going down."

"Damn right they are," I agreed.

"Hello again, everyone," the DJ said. "Are you ready to find out who the winners are tonight?"

The crowd cheered and clapped.

The DJ announced the singles winner first. I felt bad, but I honestly paid more attention to my food.

Leslie nudged my foot, and I looked up.

"Now, on to the couples," the DJ said. Someone handed him a piece of paper. "Okay, for the runner-up, we have"— he squinted and moved the paper to get more light— "Aquaman and Mera. Otherwise known as your very own Leslie Hale and her date, Asher."

I clapped but gave Leslie a sad face as she and Asher stood and waved at everyone. It appeared that Patrick and his wife had won again.

When Leslie and Asher sat, I said, "I'm sorry. I really wanted you to be the one to win."

She grinned and had that sneaky look in her eye again. "It's okay because I think I know who the winners are, and it's not Patrick and Jeanie."

Before I could ask what she was getting at, the DJ spoke

again, "And this year's winner of the couples Halloween costume contest is doctor and nurse. Otherwise known as your very own Nicholas Callan and Indy Scott."

I felt my face flush the color of Leslie's red hair as I tried to slink down in my chair.

Leslie grabbed my arm. "Stand up, Indy, and go get your prize."

I straightened. "Did you do this?"

She shrugged. "I might have had a hand in it."

"This is not funny," I hissed.

"You should see your face. It's very funny." She tilted her head to the front where Cal was already headed. "Now, go."

I stood and looked down my nose at her. "You're dead to me."

I heard my best friend laugh the whole time I was walking up to the front.

When I reached Cal, I smiled at him lamely. "I guess this is going to make it even harder to sneak around now, isn't it?"

He lifted a shoulder and smiled. "When we finally announce that you and I are a couple, we can tell them this was the night we made it official. Then, they can all look back and think, *I never knew.*"

"Does this mean we shouldn't go on a date to a restaurant of our choice?"

Cal shook his head and laughed. "I think we'd better give that to Leslie and her boyfriend to keep the gossipers at bay."

The DJ walked over with his microphone. "So, what restaurant is it going to be?"

Cal smiled. "Someone put our names down as a joke. Indy and I will not be going out to dinner together."

A few people in the crowd booed, and others laughed.

"Did you hear that?" the DJ asked us. "They want you to go have fun."

"Thanks, everyone," Cal said. "But I think we're just going to give—"

I gently elbowed Cal in the solar plexus and leaned toward the microphone. "The gift card goes to me," I finished.

"You alone?" the DJ asked with raised eyebrows.

"Yes," I said, turning my gaze toward Leslie. "Because I know who put our names down, so now, she owes me."

The crowd laughed, and I got a dinner for two at the restaurant of my choice.

TWENTY-SEVEN
INDY

I KNOCKED on the front door of the address that Cal had given me, feeling nervous for some reason. It was the first time I'd been to his house, so that had to be it. This was where I would find out if he was a slob or not. Or if he had dead bodies in the basement, as Leslie would say.

He lived in a nice neighborhood less than a half hour from my own, and his house was a little smaller than I had thought it would be. As the big boss man, I'd thought he'd have a huge home, but it was an average, middle-class size. Although it was certainly bigger than my own.

A few seconds later, I heard footsteps get closer, and the door swung open. Cal stood there in nothing but unbuttoned dark jeans and no shirt. Damn, he looked good.

I held out my flat hand. "You owe me one hundred dollars, and I've come to collect."

His brow furrowed.

"You told me that if I won the contest, you'd give me a hundred bucks."

The conversation must have come back to him because

169

he grinned as he pulled me into his house and kissed me. "How about I pay you back in orgasms?"

I shut the door behind me and pretended to think about it. "Okay, but it would be a lot faster to give me a hundred bucks now versus a hundred orgasms over the course of several days."

He raised his brow. "Days?"

"Weeks then." I wiggled my eyebrows. "Are you sure you don't want to give me the money and fulfill your commitment now?"

"No way, honey. I'm going to pay you back by making you come. Even if it takes months."

"You know I'm joking, right? I don't actually expect you to give me money."

Cal leaned down and tossed me over his shoulder, taking my overnight bag and flinging it on the floor. "I'm not." He slapped my ass. "Let the payment begin."

I squealed and laughed as he carried me up a flight of stairs, down a hall, and to a bathroom. He set me on my feet and turned on the water in his dual-showerhead stall.

"Oh, fancy," I said.

"Just wait until I fuck you under the spray. You'll wish you had a bathroom like this at home."

I ran my finger over the top of his jeans. "I don't think it matters how many showerheads I have at home if no one is there to fuck me under them."

"Good point. We'd better make sure you enjoy them here then."

He unzipped my nurse's costume, much like he had done back at the party, and cupped my breasts. "I was in such a hurry earlier that I didn't give these precious beauties much attention even though they'd been teasing me all night."

"I wore my best push-up bra just for you."

He paused and looked up at me. "Indy, did you wear this whole outfit for me?"

I lifted a shoulder. "Kind of."

"God, that is so hot."

He took my mouth and pushed off the zip-up hoodie I had thrown over my costume and then the costume itself. My bra was gone before I could help him, and so were his jeans. I hadn't put on any underwear since he'd snapped my other pair, so that was one less item of clothing to remove.

He kissed me on the way to the shower and picked me up to put me inside.

I sighed as the water hit my back and his cock entered my body.

Best shower ever.

I woke the next morning in Cal's big king-size bed, feeling refreshed and thoroughly screwed. Three down, ninety-seven orgasms to go.

Of course, I wasn't really going to keep track, but I had to tease him about it for a little bit.

I rolled over, so I was facing Cal. The blinds were shut, but there was enough light that I could see him. There was something so sexy about a guy sleeping. Especially when he was naked under the blankets.

I considered waking him up, but now was my chance to

have a peek around without him noticing. Besides, he looked so peaceful.

I slipped out of his bed and remembered that when I had packed clothes the night before, I had forgotten pajamas. I guessed I'd thought I wouldn't need them. I had been half right. I hadn't needed them to sleep, but now, I had nothing to put on.

I looked around Cal's room and found a T-shirt lying on a chair in the corner. I did a quick sniff test before I deemed it acceptable to wear. I really liked Cal, but I wasn't going to put on some stinky, sweat-filled shirt.

I tiptoed out of his room and gently shut the door behind me. Since I was already upstairs, I stuck my head into all the rooms up there. There was a bathroom that rivaled the master and two additional bedrooms besides Cal's. One of them had a bed in it. The other was mostly empty, except for a few boxes.

Downstairs, Cal had a nice, open layout with a spacious kitchen that overlooked his living room. Off the living room, he had an office with a glass door that looked kind of bare but had the essentials. His laptop was actually sitting on his kitchen counter. He also had a half-bath, which was small but efficient.

My stomach rumbled, and I was debating on whether or not to raid his fridge and pantry for food when the doorbell rang.

I spun around in a circle, much like a dog did when it chased its tail, not knowing what to do.

Hide. Or at least run upstairs and wake Cal.

Regrettably, I should have trusted my first instinct

because I was standing in plain view of the tall, skinny window next to the front door.

A woman's face appeared while I was acting like a chicken with its head cut off. She smiled when she saw me, but I froze.

It was the same woman I'd seen with Cal at Buca di Beppo.

That lying liar. Not dating anyone else? *Lies.* This woman even knew where he lived.

The woman knocked on the glass and made a *come here* motion.

I felt like crying, but it wasn't her fault that I was in the situation.

She smiled again when I started for the door, and I had a fleeting thought that she seemed awfully happy for someone who'd just caught another woman in the house of the guy she was dating.

I took a deep breath, unlocked the door, and opened it.

"Thank you," the woman said right away. "I left my keys in the car, and it's chilly out here today."

The lady had keys to his house. *Can this get any worse?*

"Chelsea," she called out as she walked inside.

"Coming," a tiny voice said, and a little girl with dark hair and green eyes came around the corner. She looked just like Cal.

Oh my God. He has a kid.

But while my brain was sounding alarms, my body stood frozen as both of them entered the house. I barely even managed to shut the door after them.

The woman set something down on the table in the entryway and reached out her hand to me. "Hi, I'm Amy."

As if on autopilot, I slowly picked up my limb and shook it. "Hi, I'm Indy." I could be freaking out inside, but the Minnesota-nice thing still shone through.

Amy smiled. "Hi, Indy." She put her hand on the girl's head. "This is Chelsea."

The child held up three fingers. "I fwee."

I stared at the little girl and wondered how Cal could have a kid who was only three when he'd lived in New York until recently. He'd said he had moved back for family. Was his daughter the family he meant? And why wasn't Amy mad that she'd found me there? I was so confused.

"Why don't you have no pants on?" Chelsea asked. "Mommy, this lady don't have no pants."

My face heated. "Oh my God. I'm so sorry."

I spun around and saw my bag on the floor where Cal had tossed it last night. I snatched it up and ran to the bathroom.

I pulled out a pair of leggings and a bra and hastily put them on. I needed to get the hell out of there before I watched Cal try to explain himself in front of the three of us.

I walked out of the bathroom just as footsteps sounded on the stairs.

I was too late.

Chelsea was standing on the couch, and her eyes lit up when she saw Cal. When he reached the bottom step, Chelsea put her foot on the back of the couch and flung herself in the air just as she shouted, "Catch me, Unca Cal."

Cal reached up and caught her with a big, "Oomph."

Chelsea giggled.

"Jeez, kid, you weigh a ton." Cal looked over at me.

"Hey, Indy, I see you've met my sister, Amy. And this little munchkin here."

I just stared at him, unable to talk. Chelsea was his *niece*. And Amy was his *sister*.

And I was the biggest idiot who had ever lived.

This was why you shouldn't fall hard and fast for a guy. You didn't know enough about him, and then you jumped to ridiculous conclusions without talking to him first.

I felt like a complete and utter moron.

TWENTY-EIGHT
INDY

CAL SET Chelsea on her feet. "Are you okay, Indy?"

Chelsea grabbed her uncle's hand. "She looks okay. But when Mommy and I got here, she didn't have no pants on."

"That's kind of my fault."

"*Cal.*" I guessed I'd found my voice.

He ignored me. "Indy had a sleepover at my house, and I forgot to buy her pajamas."

Chelsea wrinkled her nose. "Don't she have her own pajamas?"

"She does, but she left them at her house."

Chelsea looked at me. "That's not vewy smart."

"Yeah, Indy, why'd you forget your PJs?" Cal said in a teasing tone.

"Because I'm a big dummy," I said dryly.

Cal threw his head back and laughed. He took my hand. "Let's go to the kitchen. I think my sister brought doughnuts."

"Doughnuts!" Chelsea sprinted toward the kitchen.

"Hey, are you okay?" Cal asked as he headed in the

176

same direction. "You almost look like you're sick. You're pale yet flushed at the same time."

"I'm okay." Just very overwhelmed at the sudden influx of information.

"Indy, would you like a doughnut?" Amy asked. "Even though I didn't know my brother had company, I brought plenty."

My stomach was still doing flip-flops, but I didn't want to be rude, so I grabbed one. "Thank you."

"To what do I owe the visit?" Cal asked, taking a doughnut for himself.

"Chelsea and I went to church. On the way home, she said she wanted to see you. So, here I am with doughnuts."

"Aw, do you like me, munchkin?" he asked Chelsea.

She shook her head. "I wove you, Unca Cal."

"I love you too, kid."

"How long have you two been dating?" Amy asked.

I had just taken a bite of the doughnut, so Cal answered, "A few weeks."

"How did you meet?"

Cal smiled. "It's kind of a long story."

"And one I probably don't want to know," Amy said, "if that look in your eyes is anything to go by."

Cal laughed.

Amy looked at me and tilted her head. "Gosh, for some reason, you look really familiar. We haven't met before, have we?"

Oh no.

She recognized me from the night she had been with Cal. I didn't want him to know what I had suspected. Especially since I had been so wrong.

I shook my head. "No, we haven't met."

"Hmm. Man, it's going to bug me."

"Mommy, will you wash my hands?" Chelsea held out both of her hands, which were covered in chocolate.

"I'll do it," Cal said.

"Thanks, big bro."

Cal picked Chelsea up and took her over to a seat.

"What do you do for work, Indy?"

I didn't know what to say, so I went with the truth. I figured he wouldn't care if his sister knew I worked with him. "I actually work for the same company as Cal."

"Oh, really?"

"Yes, but we met before we found out we were going to work together."

"So, does that mean he's your boss?"

I looked at Cal, who was wiping his niece's fingers with a dishcloth.

"It's okay. You can tell her," Cal said.

"Yes. But we're trying to keep it on the down-low at work right now."

"You'd better be careful," Amy said toward Cal.

"I will. We're not breaking any rules, Amy. I'm going to make sure of it." Cal set Chelsea down, and the little girl ran off. He walked over to me and put his arm around me. "Besides, I really like Indy. She's totally worth it."

My face flushed again. I couldn't believe he'd just blurted out his feelings like that in front of his sister. I had just met the woman.

Amy laughed. "You should see how red you are right now."

"I can imagine."

Suddenly, Amy gasped. "Oh my God, I know where I've seen you before."

Don't say it, don't say it, don't say it. I quickly shook my head back and forth, hoping she'd get the message.

Amy looked at Cal. "Last weekend, when we went to pick up the tiramisu for Dad's birthday, remember how I told you there was a woman crouching down in the car next to me and how I thought it was weird?"

Cal leaned back and looked at me. "And it was Indy?"

I wanted to punch the grin off his face.

"It was you, wasn't it?" Amy asked.

I didn't want to lie, so I winced and said, "Yes."

"What were you doing? It looked like you were hiding."

Cal had been holding back his laughter, but at the word *hiding*, his laughter sprang out and filled the room.

"What's so funny?" Amy asked.

While it seemed Cal had figured it out, his sister had not. And I wanted to die of humiliation.

Cal clapped his hands together in apparent hilarity. "Oh my God, that's the best."

"It's not that funny," I snapped at him.

He wiped a tear from his eye. "Yes, it is."

"Tell me," Amy begged.

"Do you want to tell her?" he asked me.

"No, I don't want to tell her," I answered, horrified.

Cal shrugged and turned to Amy. "I think Indy thought I was out on a date with you."

I looked up at the ceiling. I did not want to make eye contact.

"You see, she'd been a little distant all week. Then, last

night, she said something about dating other people. Now, I know why."

"Is that true?" Amy asked.

I looked down. "I can neither confirm nor deny what happened."

Both of them started laughing now, and Cal pulled me into his arms. I immediately hid my face in his shirt.

"Do you have to be so smart?" I complained.

"You wouldn't want me any other way," he said.

"Chelsea," Amy yelled. "Come say bye to Uncle Cal and Indy. We'd better go rescue Daddy from your little brother."

Chelsea came running back in, and I stepped back, so she could hug her uncle. She gave me a high five, and Amy said goodbye to us both.

The door closed behind them, and the room was suddenly silent.

I looked at Cal. "Don't say anything, or I'll run away."

He beamed. "You like me."

"No, I don't," I yelled and ran for the stairs.

Cal's laughter sounded right behind me. When we reached his bedroom, he picked me up and threw me on the bed, landing beside me.

We were both breathing hard and staring at each other.

"I feel like a fool," I admitted to him.

"Don't. I think it's cute." He leaned down and kissed me. "Besides, I like you too."

TWENTY-NINE
CAL

MONDAY MORNING, I knew I needed to reevaluate my game plan when it came to Patrick because nothing had come of the Halloween party.

Unfortunately, since it was the beginning of the week, I had a full list of tasks I had to complete for my job.

I was just taking a break to run some numbers from all the supervisors when my phone rang.

"Hello?"

"Your mother is on the line," Keith said.

"My mother? Why didn't she call my cell?"

"I don't know. I'll put her through, so you can ask her."

The line made the clicking noise it always did when Keith transferred a call to me.

"This is Nicholas Callan."

"Cal, you sound so professional."

"Hey, Mom. I am at work, you know."

"I know."

"Why didn't you call my cell?" I cradled my phone in my ear, so I could work on my computer at the same time.

"I thought it would be better to call on your office phone."

"You don't have to. My cell is fine."

"I'll remember that for the future then."

"What's up? Why'd you call?"

She cleared her throat. "Your sister told me you had a guest over yesterday morning when she stopped by."

I sighed. "I should have known Amy would tell you right away."

"I want to meet her, Cal."

"Mom, we just started dating. I'm not sure she's ready to meet the parents yet."

"It'll just be dinner."

"It's still meeting the parents."

My mom sighed. "Will you please at least ask her?"

I stood up from my desk and looked out at the employees. Indy's cubicle was way toward the back, so I had a minimal view, but it looked like she was there.

"Give me a minute," I told my mom and picked up my cell.

> Me: My mother is on the phone right now and wants to know if you'd like to have dinner. Amy told her about you. I told her it was too soon, but she's insisting.

I saw Indy peek at me from her desk, which meant she'd probably received the text.

> Indy: I can do that. When is she thinking?

"Mom? When are you thinking?"

"How about this weekend? Can you do Saturday?"

"I'll see."

> Me: Saturday evening?

Indy: Sure. That should work.

"Mom, she said yes."

> Me: You are a saint.

My mom cheered. "Okay. Can you be at our house by six?"

"Yes. But, Mom, it's just going to be the two of us, right?"

My mom laughed. "Don't be silly. I'll invite the whole family."

"Mom, you can't do that."

Silence.

"Mom? Mom?"

The dial tone started to beep.

She'd hung up on me.

> Me: Warning: my mom is going to invite my sister, my brother-in-law, my brother, my sister-in-law, and my three nieces and nephews. You can still say no.

Indy: LOL. It's fine. I'm going to meet them eventually anyway, right?

I liked that she thought she would.

Me: Yes.

Indy: I might as well get it over with.

Me: Get it over with?

Indy: I didn't mean it like that. I'm sorry.

Me: I was kidding. I feel the same way. We might as well get it over with; otherwise, my mom will keep bugging me about it.

Indy: LOL. I'm sure it will be fine. I've met parents before.

Me: I don't want to think about that.

The thought of her meeting other guys' parents made me jealous.

Indy: We need to work on your jealousy.

Me: Are you saying you don't get jealous?

Indy: I can neither confirm nor deny that.

Me: Haha-haha. Good to know. I'd better get back to work.

Indy: Me too. Patrick keeps looking over here. I'm sure he'll bitch about me being on my phone soon. I think he's mad about the contest.

> Me: If he says anything, I want to know.

> Indy: I'll keep you updated.

> Me: Later.

> Indy: Later.

I set my phone down and went back to the numbers I had been running. I was going through each supervisors' staff and who they'd picked to head projects.

With most of them, they'd assigned each employee to be the lead quite evenly. I could tell a few had favorites, but the numbers weren't too different.

But when I got to Patrick's staff, I couldn't believe how disproportionate they were. I had only gone back the last fifty projects on each supervisor, but Patrick's showed that he had given more than eighty percent to the men on his team. He did have more men than women, so when I broke it up individually, the numbers were really sad. Indy had been the lead on three of the last fifty projects. Leslie only had two. Donna—the favorite of the three women, according to Indy —had four.

That meant the other four guys had an average of ten each.

Except when I looked again, that wasn't right either. The one black guy on Patrick's team had seven, giving the other three guys an average of eleven. This evidence was less compelling, but I still thought it was something to note.

I expanded the search to the last one hundred. I couldn't get full numbers on a couple of the supervisors because they hadn't been in their positions long enough, but I did what I could.

I came up with similar results.

I knew this wasn't enough to get Patrick out of my building, but it was a start. I was going to need more proof that he was biased.

The next thing I looked at was yearly reviews. The manager—me—was the one who did the reviews and handed out raises, but the supervisors' input was a big part of the yearly evaluation.

I got so lost in going through employee files that I didn't realize five o'clock had come and gone and that most of the staff had cleared out of the building for the day until Keith knocked on my door.

"Do you mind if I take off, Mr. Callan? It's five thirty."

I looked at my watch. "Oh, wow, I guess it is." I waved him off. "Yes, you can go."

"What about you?"

"I'll leave soon. I want to finish up on something first."

"Okay."

Keith turned.

"Keith?"

He spun back around. "Yeah, boss?"

I smiled. It wasn't Cal, but it was less professional than Mr. Callan. Maybe I'd bring Keith over to the dark side after all. "Can you make an appointment for me to meet with Patrick tomorrow?"

"I'll do it first thing in the morning."

"Thank you."

Keith walked away, and I went back to work.

THIRTY
CAL

THE NEXT MORNING, I paced my office while I waited for Patrick to arrive. I had gone over in my head how to best talk to him about my findings. I knew guys like him, and if I came out and accused him of not giving opportunities to his female employees, he would shut down and not give me anything.

I needed to get him talking and keep him talking.

But I hadn't anticipated how much of a sore loser he would be.

Patrick was always polite to me and a bit of an ass-kisser, as Indy had pointed out, but this morning, he was anything but.

"Sir, you wanted to see me?" he said from my doorway, his mouth a thin line.

"Come in and close the door, please."

Patrick walked in and stood in front of my desk, looking straight ahead. I was still off to the side, but he wouldn't turn his head my way.

I walked in front of him, so he'd be forced to meet my eyes. "Sit, please."

His mouth tightened, but he did as I'd requested. This told me he was mad that he was there, but he wasn't going to be defiant. At least, not yet.

I sat down only after Patrick had. "I wanted to talk to you about a few things."

"Okay."

"How do you pick the leaders for your projects?"

"I pick the person most likely to lead the others."

That was vague.

"Is there a reason that you give most of these positions to the men on your team?"

Patrick narrowed his eyes. "As I said, I pick the person most likely to lead."

I pulled up the piece of paper to check the numbers again before I said them out loud. "Even though most of the women on your team have more years of experience than the men?"

"Just because they have more experience doesn't mean they are the right choice."

He did have a point, but I found it hard to believe that all three were poor choices.

"Besides, it's not like the women actually want to be in charge. The only reason they work here is because two of them are single and one of them is divorced. I'm sure as soon as they get married, they will probably quit."

I stared at him, unsure that I'd heard him correctly.

"I'm sure Donna will be here forever though because no one wants to marry her. There's a reason she's divorced." Patrick smiled at me, but it came across as more of a sneer. "And I'm sure Indy will be gone soon."

I stiffened. "What makes you say that?"

"The Halloween contest. Are you two not an item? If you're not, you shouldn't have won."

The guy is this bitter over a stupid contest at a party?

"Neither I nor Indy put our names down. We didn't plan our outfits. Someone thought it was funny and probably never expected for us to actually win. If you're unhappy, you can take it up with the people who voted."

Patrick clenched his jaw.

I wanted to ask him more questions. Like, why did he always state the same information on all of his female employees' evaluations? Also, why had he never sent them to any voluntary training courses and seminars when the company had offered to pay?

But now wasn't the time. He was petty and mad at me for winning a costume contest.

"I think that's all for now."

Patrick nodded and stood. He looked down at me. "Before you ask too many questions, I think you should do a little research into who my father-in-law is."

I sat back in my chair in a relaxed pose to let him know I wasn't going to be intimidated. "You mean, Howard Brown. Yes, I'm well aware."

"Then, you're either stupid or have cojones the size of beach balls because no one is going to do anything to me. And if any employees are complaining about me, they are more likely to leave this place before me." Patrick turned on his heel and walked out.

I had to believe some of what he was saying was true,

but I also believed that no one had formally complained about him yet, so no one in Chicago knew what he was doing. I was sure they would give this guy more strikes than the average person, but at some point, they would have to pull the plug on him. He was a lawsuit waiting to happen.

And if Patrick thought I was just going to roll over and let him keep treating my employees like shit, he was in for a surprise. Maybe I was stupid, but I'd like to think it was my giant balls that had gotten me to where I was today. Because even if all my digging led to my own firing, I was going to take Patrick down with me.

I picked up my phone from my desk.

> Me: How are you? Has Patrick been giving you any crap?

> Indy: No. I think he's actually giving me the cold shoulder. I asked him a question today, and he all but ignored me. He must be really mad.

> Me: He is.

> Indy: How do you know?

> Me: I just had a meeting with him. He thinks we shouldn't have won because we're not really a couple.

> Indy: Ha. Joke's on him.

> Me: Yes, it is, but I do worry about what he'd do if he knew.

Indy: What did you find out from HR?

I'd been so busy yesterday that I'd forgotten to look at the employee manual, so it was the first thing I'd done when I arrived at work this morning.

Me: There are no rules saying employees who work together can't date. And as long as I'm not your immediate supervisor, it's okay.

Indy: That's great news.

I grinned at my phone.

Me: Yes, it is.

Indy: So, how much longer are we going to sneak around? Not that I'm complaining, but I've barely seen you the last few days.

Me: Sorry. I've been busy. And people might suspect if I have a personal meeting with you every day.

Indy: Damn, you're right. What about tonight?

Me: After the two days I've had, I want nothing more than to be naked with you tonight.

Indy: My place or yours?

Me: Whoever lives closer.

I waited a few seconds for Indy to respond.

Indy: I just looked it up. I live three minutes closer.

Me: Your house it is.

Indy: You bring dinner. I'll bring dessert. ;-)

Me: How does Buca di Beppo sound?

Indy: Never mind. You're uninvited. You can get naked with yourself tonight.

I laughed, not caring if people looked into my office and wondered what I was doing.

Me: Okay, I apologize for teasing you. I'll get food from somewhere else.

Indy: Apology accepted, but just know that I added a few more orgasms to the ones you already owe me. It's back up to one hundred.

Me: One hundred? I'll never pay them off.

Indy: That's the idea.

Grinning, I set my phone down, feeling much better than I had when Patrick left my office.

THIRTY-ONE
INDY

SATURDAY NIGHT WAS COMING UP FAST, and I was starting to get really anxious. In my head, I knew it wasn't going to be a big deal. I'd already met Cal's sister, and she'd seemed to like me. He'd assured me his mom would like me too.

But while I tried to tell myself it was going to be a no-big-deal dinner, I couldn't shake the nerves.

I needed to do something to clear my head because watching TV wasn't doing it for me.

I looked over into Cal's office where he had gone since the noise from the television was bugging him. He was wearing a plain white T-shirt and jeans with no socks. Such a simple look but one of my favorites.

Add that to the serious expressions on his face as he studied what was on his screen, and I couldn't stop thinking about how sexy he was. I wanted to eat him up.

Inspiration struck, and I pulled up my phone and scrolled back through our messages.

This was just the distraction I needed.

I walked to his office door and hesitated for a moment. I didn't know if he would be bothered by me interrupting him. But I had a feeling he'd be more than happy to live out his little fantasy and would forgive me for any disruption.

I knocked, and he lifted his head, so I opened the door.

He smiled. "Hey, what's up? I'm almost done here."

I didn't say anything, just dropped to my knees.

Cal's brow furrowed in confusion. "What are you doing?"

I crawled toward him in what I hoped was a seductive way. I was channeling Baby from *Dirty Dancing* and aimed to portray that kind of sexiness.

A grin split across Cal's face as I rounded his desk, and he turned his chair, so he faced me.

When I reached him, I ran my hands up his legs and went straight for his fly. I wasn't quite under his desk, but I thought we both knew how crowded that would be. Plus, we were in his house. We didn't need to hide anything.

I pulled the button and unzipped his jeans, making sure my finger rubbed the length of his shaft at the same time. I tugged his jeans and boxers down just enough for me to get to the thing I wanted most, and I pulled out his cock.

Cal hissed as I squeezed him in my hand. He was big and beautiful. God had certainly blessed him in the penis department.

Pre-cum leaked from the tip, and I looked up into his eyes as I sucked it off.

"Fuck, baby," he muttered.

I licked around the head and drew him into my mouth with a light suction.

Cal's hips arched off the chair, and I had to stop myself from smiling. I didn't want to hurt him with my teeth.

I kissed and licked and sucked on him for a few minutes, enjoying the taste of him and the reactions I was getting out of him. When I felt he'd had enough teasing, I wrapped one hand around the base of him and began to pump.

Cal's hand came up to cup the back of my head, and his fingers threaded in my hair. But he didn't push my head down or force me to do anything. It was as if he just wanted to feel me, which fueled my desire.

I considered reaching down and touching myself, but that wasn't a part of Cal's fantasy, so I kept my hands on him instead.

Soon, I knew he was close to orgasm. His breathing picked up, and he seemed to have a hard time keeping his hips still. I felt him grow thicker in my mouth until he exploded on my tongue. I swallowed all of him until he grew sensitive and tried to pull away.

I began to tuck him back into his pants when he picked me up and practically threw me on his desk. Not in a violent way, but in a *I have to have you now* way.

He wasted no time in pulling my own jeans off my legs and shoving his face between my thighs. My butt was on the edge of his desk and my feet on the arms of his chair. He pushed my thighs open wide, as it was his turn to lick and suck everywhere.

I wanted this feeling to last forever, but I had already been at an eleven out of ten when he put me on his desk after I gave him a blow job. Before, I would never have complained about coming too fast, but they said there was a first time for everything.

I tried to hold it off, but my orgasm hit my core, much like I imagined a punch would feel to my face.

I cried out and tried to make it last, but it was all over too soon.

Cal stood and pushed down his pants. "Did you cry out no?"

I stuck out my lower lip. "I wasn't ready to come yet," I said with a pout.

He chuckled. "I've never heard that complaint before." He pushed my knees up, spreading me wide. "Good thing we're not done." He licked his fingers, ran them over the head of his cock, and thrust inside me to the hilt.

My breath caught at the pinch of pain from being filled so full, so fast, but it subsided within seconds.

Cal fell over my body and lifted my shirt. He yanked down my bra and sucked one nipple into his mouth as he fucked me.

I grabbed the back of his head and neck and wrapped my legs around his back. Everything he was doing felt incredible. From his thumbs digging into my hips to the way he moved inside me.

"Oh my God," I cried out. "Not again." *What is wrong with me today?* There were times when I couldn't come a second time, and today, I couldn't stop coming too fast.

Cal moved to my other breast and made his thrusts shallower as he slowed his pace. I didn't like this either. I wanted to feel him as deeply as I could.

I ran my hands down his back and scratched him with my nails. "No. Don't stop."

He lifted his head and looked into my eyes as he slowly —too slowly—gave me all of himself again.

He hit all the right spots inside me, and I began to see stars. This time, I didn't care that I was going to come again so soon because it felt too good. I closed my eyes, letting the tingles in my body wash over me.

Cal grabbed on to my hair and tugged. "Watch me."

I blinked my eyes open.

"I want you to watch me while you come."

I'd never had an orgasm with my eyes open as far as I could remember. I shook my head.

"Yes. You can do it."

I shook my head again. *No, I can't.*

"Yes, you can, baby. I want you to come for me."

My pussy started to pulse.

Cal nodded. "That's it. Come now. Let go."

The dam broke, and I cried out at the force of my climax.

Cal tugged on my hair again. "Keep them open, Indy."

I stared into Cal's eyes as I let him see me in that incredibly vulnerable moment.

Cal slammed his hips into me a couple more times but kept his eye contact as his own orgasm took ahold of his body.

When we were both spent and shaking, Cal put his forehead on mine.

I enveloped him in my arms and hung on tight, just enjoying the feel of him so close to me.

I had never felt so exposed yet treasured in my entire life.

THIRTY-TWO
INDY

CAL PICKED up my hand as we walked to the front door of his parents' house. Our incredible lovemaking session had calmed my nerves for a little bit, but they were back and stronger than ever.

"Indy, it's going to be okay. My parents are not picky about who I date. As long as I'm happy, they're happy. They've been waiting for me to bring someone home for some time."

I looked at him in horror. "You haven't ever brought anyone home?" I didn't want to be the first.

"Yes, I have. But it's been a long time. I think my mother has given up on her oldest child ever getting married."

"*Married*? They think we're getting married?"

Cal laughed. "No, they don't think that. I'm simply trying to put the relationship into perspective for you. They're going to be happy that I'm bringing you over. So happy that they aren't going to judge you."

"I'll believe it when I see it," I said as we reached the entrance.

Cal laughed, knocked, and opened the door. "Mom, Dad? We're here."

We came in through the back from the garage and entered the kitchen where something smelled delicious. No one was in the room, and I took a deep breath as I heard the sound of small feet fast approaching.

"Unca Cal," Chelsea shouted as she rounded the corner.

"Hey, kiddo," he said, picking her up.

Amy came into the kitchen first, followed by an older woman who looked like Amy and an older man who looked a lot like Cal.

The woman, who had to be Cal's mom, stepped forward and held out her hand. "Hello, Indy. We're so glad you're here. I'm Joanne Callan, but you can call me Jo."

I smiled at her warm welcome and shook her hand. "Hi, Jo."

Jo let go of my hand, and the man, who had to be Cal's dad, stepped forward and held out his hand. "Hello there. I'm Nick."

His greeting was also warm, and I did a quick study of the man who Cal had been named after. I wondered how much Cal would look like Nick when he got older because the man looked good for his age.

"And you know my sister, Amy, and my favorite niece, Chelsea."

Cal tickled her belly, and the little girl giggled.

"She's your only niece," Amy pointed out.

"That doesn't mean she's not my favorite."

Jo motioned us forward. "Come in, you two. Let me take your coat, Indy."

"Oh, thank you," I said as I slid out of my jacket and handed it to her.

Cal set Chelsea down and took off his own coat. "Here you go, Mom."

Jo looked at Cal, then his coat, and then at Cal again. "You know where to hang it up, son," she said and walked away.

I put my hand over my mouth and stifled a laugh as everyone walked out of the kitchen.

Cal leaned over. "See? I told you, nothing to worry about."

We followed everyone into the living room where a man sat, holding a little boy.

"Indy, this is my husband, Jon, and this is Bobby."

Jon stood and shook my hand.

"How old is Bobby?" I asked.

"Almost ten months."

I gave the baby a finger wave. "Hi, Bobby."

He smiled at me, and I grinned.

"Do you have any nieces, nephews…kids?" Jo asked.

"Mom," Cal said.

I laughed. "No kids of my own. I do have a niece and a nephew, but they don't live close. I grew up in a small town about four hours from here. My dad is a farmer, and so is my brother, so that's where all of my family lives. Not many software companies out there though, so here I am."

Cal put his arm around me. "I bet."

"It's okay though. I always wanted to live somewhere bigger. I came for college and never moved back."

Cal shuddered. "Ugh. Small towns. I don't blame you."

"Yeah, I bet, Mr. New York."

Lights flashed across the front window as a car pulled into the driveway.

"That must be your brother," Jo said.

Cal looked down at me. "I'm sorry you have to meet everyone at once. I told my mom to make it just the four of us, but she doesn't listen."

Jo waved Cal away. "Pishposh. Rip off the bandage, I say."

"That's just an excuse. My mom can't invite just one child over."

Nick started laughing, and Jo scowled at him.

"Cal is not wrong," Nick stated.

Jo lifted her hands in surrender. "I love my family. Sue me."

I had a huge smile on my face as we waited for Cal's brother and family to come into the house. Cal had been right. I had nothing to worry about. They were down-to-earth, and if I had to take a guess, I would say they liked me.

"Why don't you have a seat, Indy?" Jo said. "We don't all have to stand here like we're waiting for them to enter."

"Good point," Cal said and led me over to the couch. "My brother already thinks he's better than me," he told me.

"Oh, he does not," Jo said and walked into the kitchen.

"Does he really?" I asked in a low voice.

Cal laughed. "Nah. My mom just hates any sibling rivalry, so I like to rile her up."

"You must have been a joy to raise."

Cal laughed as a mix of voices came from the kitchen. A woman and another little boy walked into the room.

"Indy, this is Dana, my daughter-in-law. And Oliver, my grandson."

I stood and shook Dana's hand and sat back down. "Hi, Oliver."

Oliver smiled but hid behind his mom's leg.

"How old?" I asked.

"Fourteen months."

"That's nice that Oliver and Bobby can play with each other."

"Yeah, once Bobby starts walking, there will be no stopping the two of them," Amy said.

I smiled, picturing Cal and me having a child to add to the mix, and I startled myself with the thought.

Cal put his hand on my knee. "You okay?" he asked me in a low voice.

I smiled at him. "Yes. Just thinking some good thoughts."

"I hope it was about me."

"Oh, it was."

He squeezed my knee and grinned.

"Indy?"

I looked up to Jo.

"The last person I'm going to introduce you to tonight, I promise, is Cal's brother, Joel."

Alarm bells went off in my head, and my smile disappeared.

Joel? There was no way it could be the same Joel.

But then I looked at Cal, and my stomach dropped. That was how I'd gotten his number that night. Joel had given me his brother's instead of his own.

I held my breath, hoping I was wrong until Cal's brother

walked into the living room. My *oh shit* moment was suddenly very real.

"Joel, this is Indy, Cal's new friend."

Joel halted for a second, but then he smiled and stepped forward. "Hi, Indy. Nice to meet you."

I shook his hand and had to resist wiping my palm on my pants.

I looked at Dana and little Oliver and then at Cal. He looked so happy. I had no idea how I was going to tell Cal that his brother was a big, fat cheater.

THIRTY-THREE
CAL

"I THINK THAT WENT GREAT," I told Indy as we drove back to my house. "I knew you had nothing to worry about."

She smiled at me, but it didn't quite reach her eyes. I hoped she didn't think my family was insincere because I could tell they all liked her. My brother had been a little distant, but I'd noticed he'd been off lately.

It was something I should maybe ask him about, but he and I had never been close. I'd always been closer to Amy.

When we got home, I pulled Indy into the bedroom and started kissing her. She surprised me by putting her hand on my chest and gently pushing me away.

She took a deep breath. "We need to talk."

Nothing ever good came after those words.

"Okay."

"Can we sit?"

I grabbed her hand and led her over to the bed. "What's wrong?"

She drew her hand from mine and looked away. "I don't know how to tell you this."

I was starting to get concerned now. We'd had a great afternoon. And tonight had been a success. "Did meeting my family happen too fast? I know we'd only started talking about not sleeping with other people."

"No. It's not that."

"Then, what is it?" I put a finger under her chin and turned her face my way. "You can tell me."

She pulled her head away. "You remember how we met, right?"

I grinned. "How could I forget?" I thought I realized what was bothering her. "Are you worried about what to tell people about how we met? We don't have to tell them we had wild monkey sex together right away. We can always say we kept texting each other."

That got a half-smile out of her. "No, it's not that. But it is something to consider. Thankfully, your parents didn't ask how we'd met."

"Okay. If it's not that, then what is it?"

"The guy that I was seeing from the dating app…the one who gave me your phone number…"

"What about him?"

"I don't think it was a random number." She huffed out a laugh. "No. I know it wasn't a random number."

"What are you getting at?" I was genuinely confused.

She looked at me and met my eyes. "The guy I was seeing…his name was Joel."

I frowned and shook my head. "You think that someone used my brother's name and gave you my phone number?"

She smiled at me, her eyes still a little sad. "Finally, some proof that you're not always the smartest in the room."

"Not by a long shot. Please explain."

"No one was pretending to be your brother, Cal. Your brother is who I went on three dates with."

I sat, stunned, for a minute. "But he's married."

"I know. I'm guessing that's why he gave me your phone number."

I looked at Indy and pictured my brother on a date with her. Kissing her. Making love to her.

I jumped up from the bed and began pacing the room. I didn't like this feeling coursing through my body. I'd thought I was jealous of Indy's date at the Halloween party, but it was nothing compared to how I felt about my brother.

I stopped and ran my hands down my face. "I know I have no right to ask this, but..." I took a deep breath. "How *involved* with my brother did you get?"

"Three dates. He only ever kissed me." She held up her hands. "Pecks."

I breathed the biggest sigh of relief.

Indy raised her eyebrows. "It's still cheating, Cal."

"Right. Yes, I know."

"Are you mad at me? Because I suspected he had a girl-friend after he gave me the wrong number, but I'd had no idea up until then. I'd thought he just wanted to take things slow."

I pulled her up toward me and enveloped her in my arms. "No, I'm not mad at you."

"Good, because I don't mess with other women's men. I do feel stupid though. What kind of man wants to take things that slow?"

I lifted her chin. "Indy, this is not on you. This is on my brother." I thought about his wife. "What a dick. Dana probably has no clue."

"What do we do now?"

I shook my head. "I don't know." I looked her in the eyes. "But I don't want you to do anything. I will take care of this. He's my brother."

"I'm sorry I had to be the bearer of such bad news." She put her head on my chest. "What a way to ruin a good day."

"Honey, it's not your fault."

"Do you want me to go home? I'll understand if you do."

I squeezed her to me. "Hell no."

After I did a little more processing, I was going to make love to her all night. I was going to make sure she and I both knew who she belonged to because even though nothing had happened between her and Joel, I couldn't stop thinking about them being together.

I pulled away. "Why don't you get ready for bed?"

She nodded. "Okay," she said and turned to walk away.

I yanked her back and gave her a deep kiss. "Just so you know I mean it."

She smiled and headed to the bathroom.

While she was in there, I went out to the kitchen to grab my phone and brought it back to the bedroom. "What's the name of the app?" I asked Indy through the open door.

The water in the sink shut off, and she gave me the name of the popular app. I downloaded it onto my phone and opened it. But I had no account, and going on as myself was not going to help me find my brother.

Indy walked out of the bathroom, and I forgot all about my phone, the app, and my brother.

"Come here," I said and spread my legs.

She stepped between them and ran her fingers through my hair. "Are you going to be okay?"

I lifted her shirt and kissed her belly. "I will be once I'm inside you." I picked her up and threw her on the bed. As I crawled up her body, I looked down at her. "I need you tonight, Indy."

She nodded, opened her arms, and took all of me.

THIRTY-FOUR
CAL

THE NEXT MORNING, Indy woke up to me staring at my phone.

She did a double take when she saw what app I was on. "What are you doing?"

"Making an account."

She sat up. "Are you going to catfish your own brother?"

"Thinking about it. When I confront him, I want to have proof that I can literally shove in his face." I looked at Indy. "Do you still have your conversations with him on your phone?"

She shook her head. "I deleted them all and blocked him. I could unblock him, but I'm sure he'd block me in return right away, if he hasn't already."

"Yeah, you're right. For all we know, he deleted his whole account."

"That would be the smart thing to do. Does that mean you're not going to make an account?"

I shook my head. "I'm making an account. I have to see it for myself."

"I understand."

"Now, what should my name be?'"

She smiled. "Callie."

I laughed. "You're funny. And I meant, my username."

"Thanks. And pick anything. Whatever you use, you'll have to add a bunch of numbers behind it because only a name will most likely already be taken. What you need are some good pictures to lure him in."

"Crap. I didn't even think about that."

"I'll send you some of Leslie."

"You're going to use your friend's pics to help me catfish my brother?"

"You can't use mine. And don't worry; I'll warn her."

I looked over at her. "You're the perfect partner in crime."

She put a finger to her lips and smiled. "Shh...don't tell anyone."

Monday morning at work, I couldn't stop thinking about my brother, to the point that I couldn't focus on my current project.

I kept scrolling through the app on my phone, looking for him. Indy had helped me put in similar info that she had entered so that I'd get my brother as a match. So far, I hadn't found him. I hoped that he had realized how much he'd screwed up and gone home and deleted the app on Saturday night, yet I couldn't stop searching for him.

I had no idea what I would do when or if I did find him. Should I tell my sister-in-law? Should I talk to my brother first? Should I tell my brother he needed to come clean? Should I talk to my mother and father about it and let them decide? All I knew was I did not want this responsibility.

There was a knock at my office door.

I turned my screen off and set my phone down. "Come in."

Keith opened it and stepped inside before shutting the door.

He looked serious, and I welcomed the distraction.

"What's going on?"

Keith pointed his thumb behind him. "Aaron wants to talk to you. He looks worried."

"Send him in."

Aaron Fredricks was one of the supervisors who worked under me, and I liked the guy. I had gotten good vibes from him when I first met with him, and his team seemed to really like him.

Keith opened the door and let Aaron in.

"Thanks, Keith," I told him.

Keith stepped out and closed the door behind him.

"Have a seat, Aaron. What can I do for you?"

Aaron sat down and immediately began pumping his leg up and down, looking nervous. "I want you to know that I'm not normally a tattletale or a snitch."

"Aaron, there is a difference between tattling and telling. If someone is doing something that I need to know about, that is telling."

Aaron smiled. "Good way to word that."

"Thank you." I'd heard Amy telling Chelsea that once. Who knew it would be relevant at work too?

Aaron rubbed his hands together, and I could tell he was still nervous.

"How about you give me the info in hypotheticals and not use any names? Then, if I feel like it isn't important, we can pretend we never had this conversation."

Aaron nodded. "Okay. That works."

"So, what is your hypothetical situation?"

"I have this coworker who I mostly tolerate. We're not friends, but we're not enemies."

I nodded. I'd been there a couple of times.

"Sometimes, this person says things that are inappropriate, but I ignore them and move on with my day."

"Okay," I said. "You'll probably have to be more specific because, let's face it, everyone says inappropriate things at work. If I fired everyone for saying things they shouldn't have, I wouldn't have any employees. Including myself." I'd said some very inappropriate things to Indy at work.

"This person always makes statements that walk the line of what's unsuitable in the workplace. However, in the last week, he's said some things that have made me very uncomfortable."

"Can you give me some examples?"

Aaron looked down at the floor. "He said that...a certain female was a...S-L-U-T for black...penises. After you confronted him about a few things, he also said that another female was sucking your...penis. But then he also said that you probably didn't like it because you'd rather be the one to...suck penis."

My jaw clenched, and I wanted to punch something. Or someone. But I didn't want Aaron to think I was mad at him.

Aaron looked up at me. "I want you to know that I don't approve of his behavior—at all. I have two sisters and...a boyfriend."

"Does Patrick know you're gay?"

Aaron shook his head. "I don't think so. Maybe." He shrugged. "I don't advertise it, but I also don't hide it."

"Still doesn't make it okay even if you were straight," I added.

"How did you know it was Patrick?" Aaron asked.

"I had a hunch. I'm guessing the women you're talking about are Leslie and Indy. He seems to be really bitter about losing the Halloween contest." I shook my head. "I don't get it. It's just a stupid contest."

"Patrick can't stand when someone does better than him. At anything. Rumor has it that he got Colby sick—gave him food poisoning—after Polly announced that Colby was going to Arizona for a conference. So, Patrick got to go instead. No one could ever prove it though."

"Have you brought your concerns to HR?"

Aaron shook his head. "No. I know who his father-in-law is. I probably wouldn't have even said something to you, except you'd just had those classes and told us we could come to you about anything." He looked sheepish. "Plus, this time, it was personal. I know that's horrible to say. It honestly did make me uncomfortable when he said those things about Leslie and Indy. But it really cuts to the bone when someone says something about your own lifestyle."

"I guess that's a lesson to us all that just because someone doesn't say something about a certain group, it doesn't mean they don't think things or say things to other people. That's why we all need to look out for each other. One day, it's them; the next day, it's you."

Aaron nodded again, his eyes full of guilt. "You're right."

"The good thing is, you're here now. You did the right thing by speaking up."

"What do you want me to do from here? Do you want me to go to HR?"

"No. With Patrick's father-in-law's position, I'm going to take everything I have on the guy to HR myself. I need you to write a statement of what you heard. Only include things you heard directly. And please make sure you write down the actual words that were used. I'm guessing you made it more PG-13 for me. I want HR to get the R-rated version."

"I can do that."

"Last thing, if you know of anyone else who feels like you do, please have them come to me. The more statements I have, the stronger the case."

Aaron stood. "Will do, boss."

We said goodbye, and I got to work on plans for bringing my information on Patrick to HR. This was going to have to be handled with a lot of finesse.

THIRTY-FIVE

INDY

CAL and I hadn't talked much the last two days. He'd been staying late at work and then doing whatever life errands he needed to do before coming over to my house. By the time he got there, he usually took me to bed and made love to me before we both fell asleep.

I could tell he had a lot on his mind, so I didn't bother him by asking a bunch of questions. Plus, having sex with me seemed to be his stress reliever. I wasn't going to take that away from him. Especially when he took care of my needs too.

But I knew he couldn't keep everything bottled up inside forever, so I camped out in one of the private rooms while I waited for everyone else to leave. It took longer than expected because Keith liked to stick around as long as the boss did. I was getting pretty bored of playing games on my phone when I finally heard Keith leave.

I watched Cal through the glass windows of his office as I approached. He rubbed his forehead, looking tense, and my heart went out to him.

I knocked on the doorjamb.

"Keith, I said you could go home," he said without even looking up.

"I'm not Keith."

His head whipped up, and he smiled. The smile reached his green eyes, but he looked exhausted.

"Hey, are you okay?" I asked as I stepped inside.

"Are we alone?" he asked.

"It's just you and me."

He opened his arms and twisted his seat sideways. "Come here then."

I walked around to his side of the desk and got on his lap.

He tucked my head under his chin and rubbed my back.

"Are you okay?" I asked again.

He sighed. "No."

I sat up and ran my thumb over his cheek. "What's wrong, handsome?"

He smiled wearily at my compliment.

"Is it your brother?"

He snorted. "I haven't even had time to think about Joel since Monday. No, I have to go back to Chicago."

I frowned. "Again? Why?"

"I contacted HR about Patrick, and now, they want me to come there. I have a meeting with them on Friday."

Cal had kept me up-to-date on Patrick. I didn't know all the details, but I knew he felt he had solid evidence to take to HR.

"You can't just talk over the phone? Or have a video conference?"

He shrugged. "I guess not. They said it was something they needed to discuss in person."

"That doesn't sound good. Do you think you're in trouble?"

Cal looked like he was searching for the right words. "I don't think trouble per se, but they might be worried that I'm making waves where they don't want them."

"Ugh...I hate nepotism."

Cal smiled. "What you and I have could be called nepotism."

I kissed him. "But there's a big difference. I'm a good worker, I'm not an asshole, and I was here before you; you didn't hire me."

He kissed me long and deep, his hands running all over my body. When he pulled away, we were both breathing hard. "God, I love it when you say such smart things." He kissed my neck. "Thanks for not being an asshole, by the way. I wouldn't want to worry about firing your sweet ass too."

I laughed and melted into his touch. "You keep that up, and we're going to have another naughty session in your office."

Cal groaned and leaned back on his chair. "As much as I'd love to be inside you right now, I'd probably better finish up my work. I wasn't prepared to go to Chicago at the last minute. I'm trying to get ahead of things."

"When are you leaving?"

"Tomorrow afternoon."

"Does that mean you're coming over tonight?"

"I need to pack. Would you mind going to my house instead?"

I shook my head. "I'll go home and grab a few things. What time should I come over?"

"You can go over right away. I'm not sure how long I'll be." He opened up his desk drawer, pulled out his keys, and took one off the ring. "Here. Use this to get in."

"Ooh…a key to your house. This is getting serious," I joked.

Cal didn't say anything. He just cupped my face, pulled me close, and kissed me again. "Okay, you need to get out of here, so I can finish. That way, I'll be that much closer to getting home to you."

I smiled. I liked how he called being with me home. "Don't you need your key?"

"I use my garage door opener."

I got up from his lap, took the key, and kissed him again. "I'll see you there."

I went to my desk and grabbed my purse before looking at Cal one more time. I felt bad for him. He was worried about work and about his brother. Struck with inspiration as I walked to the elevators, I pulled up my phone and put in an order for someone to deliver him some food.

My man needed to eat if he was going to take care of business.

When I reached the hallway, I saw the doors to the elevator close, which was weird. I couldn't tell if anyone had been in there though. Maybe someone had accidentally pushed our floor, and it had stopped here.

I pushed the down button and finished Cal's food order.

By the time I got to Cal's house, he texted me.

Cal: I got the food. Thank you.

Me: You're welcome. But I did it for purely selfish reasons. I need you in full form if you're going to give me a proper goodbye fucking.

Cal: Ha-ha. I knew it. You just want me for my dick.

Me: Guilty.

Me: Seriously though, if you're going to go to Chicago and meet with them, you need to be at your best. Please promise me you'll be home early, so you can get a good night's sleep.

Cal: So, no goodbye fucking?

Me: I guess that depends on what time you get home.

Cal: I'll be there in an hour. Hour and a half, tops.

Cal got to his house within two hours, which was better than I'd expected. We slipped into bed, had phenomenal goodbye sex, and still went to sleep at a decent time.

When I woke up, I was alone because Cal had already gone to work. He wanted to get things done there before he went to the airport after lunch. I was disappointed that I hadn't gotten to say goodbye again that morning. Not a sexual goodbye. I'd simply wanted him to hold me for a bit since I wouldn't see him for a few days.

I knew he'd be back, but I couldn't shake my sadness. I

dismissed my melancholy as my period coming any day now. At least I would have it while he was out of town.

And when Cal came back, I was going to give him a proper welcome home.

THIRTY-SIX
CAL

MY PLANE LANDED in Chicago around five on Thursday evening, and I didn't have to be at the Chicago office until eight the next morning.

I wish I had flown in later to spend some more time with Indy before leaving, but I wasn't the one who had scheduled my flight. The Chicago office had.

And I couldn't shake the ominous feeling hanging over me.

I had downplayed the situation with Indy, but I knew it wasn't a good that I had been all but ordered to come there. The Minneapolis office wasn't big, so all our HR people were in Chicago. Chicago was at least double the size of Minneapolis. Their reasoning was that HR could be done using technology. But then why couldn't I discuss my findings over the phone?

When I'd first called HR, the woman I had spoken with was receptive and open to listening to the transgressions I listed. But the minute I gave her a name, I heard a change in her voice, and she told me she would have to get back to me. Thirty minutes later, she had emailed me with my flight information. It was a bad sign that she hadn't even bothered to call me back.

That night, I tried to go to bed early, but I tossed and turned before falling into a fitful sleep.

The next morning, I made it to the Chicago office early since I couldn't sleep anyway, but I was left sitting around all day. The secretary kept coming up with lame excuses every time I asked when I would go into my meeting. Finally, at three thirty in the afternoon—seven and a half hours later —I was told to come back on Monday at eight.

I went in search of food because I hadn't gotten to eat all day and weighed my options. I knew that management was sending a message to me. They probably had never intended to meet with me until Monday. They wanted to show me who had the power.

I didn't want Indy to worry, so I told her there had been an illness and that I would miss her.

Monday, I went in early again—this time, armed with snacks in case I was left waiting again all day. I was led back into a conference room about twenty minutes after my appointment.

When I entered the room, I was greeted by the CEO of the company, George Malone; the president, Shane Randu; a woman and an older gentleman I didn't recognize; and Patrick, looking like a smug son of a bitch.

I was being ambushed.

The woman stood and held out her hand. "Nicholas Callan? I'm Alice."

Alice was the HR woman I had spoken to.

"Alice Geer," I said in greeting.

"You know Mr. Malone and Mr. Randu?" she asked.

I nodded. "Hello again."

"This is Howard Brown, and you know Patrick Mullen." She pointed to an open chair. "Please, have a seat, Mr. Callan."

Despite being surrounded by everyone in power, I took my seat, opened my briefcase, and removed the information I had on Patrick.

"You're not going to need any of that, young man," Howard said when he saw my pile of papers.

"Sir, I respectfully disagree. If you give me a chance to show you the information I've acquired, you will see that——"

Howard held up his hand and interrupted me, "Ms. Geer has already filled me in." He pointed to the CEO and president. "Us in."

"I see," I said.

They wanted me to know that they had heard enough and didn't want to hear any more. It didn't matter what proof I had.

"Patrick has agreed to transfer back to Chicago. He will no longer have anyone working under him, so as far as the board, Mr. Malone, and Mr. Randu are concerned, this matter is taken care of. And we hope you are on the same page as us." Howard Brown gave me a look that dared me to challenge him.

Message received.

"Yes, I am on the same page."

I was sure that whatever new position they put Patrick in, it was probably going to be an improvement from his former job. That was just how these things worked.

I looked around the room and met everyone's eyes.

"Why then did you feel the need to fly me here? You certainly could have told me all this during a conference call."

Howard Brown nodded at Patrick, who pulled out a large manila envelope and slid it over to me.

"Go ahead," Howard said. "Open it."

Dread filled my gut as I broke the seal. When I pulled out the pictures of Indy sitting on my lap at work, the feeling moved into my throat.

This had to be from Wednesday night when Indy and I had thought we were alone. That sneaky asshole had waited around just to catch us. I had to wonder how long he'd been spying on the two of us.

"As you can see, you're not the only one who has brought concerns to us. There are more pictures of the two of you at each other's homes, but we figured these images were sufficient."

I slammed the pictures down. "I checked into the employee manual. The only relationships that are frowned upon are anyone involved with their direct supervisor." I looked at Patrick. "Lucinda Scott's direct supervisor is Patrick." Or had been Patrick.

Howard gave an expectant look to the CEO and president.

Mr. Malone cleared his throat. "As of this morning, we are promoting Lucinda Scott to fill Mr. Mullen's position as the supervisor of her team. You will now be her direct supervisor." Mr. Malone looked uncomfortable, and I felt he was on my side.

Mr. Randu wouldn't meet my eyes, and I sensed he felt

the same. Unfortunately, both of them answered to the board.

And I had to hand it to Howard Brown. He could have demoted me to Patrick's position, but instead, he was promoting Indy. It would be hard to make a lawsuit out of getting a better position with better pay.

Howard Brown knew he had me where he wanted me. And so did Patrick. The smugness on both bastards' faces made me want to punch them, but I wasn't going to give them any more power over me.

I picked up my now-worthless reports and shoved them in my briefcase. The sense of defeat was overwhelming, especially after all that time I'd wasted.

"Mr. Callan?"

I looked up at Howard Brown.

"You have until the end of the week to decide what you'd like to do. Either break things off with Ms. Scott or fire her. The choice is yours."

I stood and looked Howard in the eyes. "I pick neither. Consider this my resignation. Effective immediately."

I heard Alice gasp as I picked up my briefcase and walked out of the room.

They had played their last hand and lost. I wasn't going to fire Indy, and I certainly wasn't going to give her up. And I certainly didn't want to work for a company that would make me choose.

THIRTY-SEVEN
INDY

MONDAY MORNING STARTED the same as usual, except that Cal wasn't there. He was supposed to have come back on Saturday, but someone in Chicago had gotten sick, so they'd had to reschedule his meeting.

I was feeling nervous. His meeting should have started at eight. It was almost nine now, and I hadn't heard anything yet. I had waited all day on Friday for Cal to go into his meeting, only to have it rescheduled. I didn't know if I could take a whole other day like that today. I was sure to have a stroke from my blood pressure being high.

I tapped away on my computer but found it hard to concentrate. I picked up my phone for the fiftieth time. No message since I had wished Cal good luck at seven forty-five that morning.

I was still staring off into space when Keith came up to me.

"Indy, I need you to come to Cal's office," he said in almost a whisper.

I quickly turned to glance at Leslie.

"No. You can't tell anyone."

"What's this about?" I asked in an equally low voice.

My first thought was that Cal had gotten into an accident or was hurt. My stomach was in knots.

"I don't know. They didn't tell me anything." He tilted his head toward the office. "Come on. Let's go."

Keith turned his back to me, so I snuck a quick look at Leslie. Of course, she had been paying attention the whole time. I shrugged at her and hurried after Keith.

Once in Cal's office, he went behind Cal's desk and pushed a few buttons on the computer. He stood straight. "Okay, they're ready for you."

"Who is?"

Keith came around to my side and leaned in close. "The CEO and president."

My eyes widened, and I swallowed. This couldn't be good.

"Good luck," Keith whispered as he exited the room.

I hesitantly walked around to the front of the computer.

"Hello, Ms. Scott," Mr. Randu said. "Please have a seat."

I pulled out Cal's chair but didn't say a word.

"There are going to be a lot of rumors flying around the office in a few minutes," Mr. Malone said.

That didn't explain why they had pulled me—a nobody —into the office for a private conversation.

"Is Cal okay?" I asked.

The two men exchanged looks, and my breath caught.

Mr. Randu must have sensed my worry. "Mr. Callan is fine—physically. He just left our office about ten minutes ago."

I put my hand to my chest and took a deep breath. "Thank you."

"Unfortunately, Mr. Callan no longer works for us," the president said.

My temporary relief was gone. "What?"

I can't believe they fired him. He had done nothing wrong.

"Yes," Mr. Malone said. "Mr. Callan submitted his resignation as of this morning. Effective immediately."

Cal quit?

My brain was so stunned that I almost missed their next words.

"Also, as of today, Patrick Mullen is being transferred back to Chicago, and you are going to take over his position."

I held up my hand. "I'm sorry. Can you repeat that?"

"You are now the supervisor of your team. Mr. Mullen is not coming back to Minneapolis," Mr. Randu said. "We're going to be sending out an email soon to let everyone know."

I shook my head. "Shouldn't I have to apply for this spot? There might be others who are more qualified."

The two traded looks again.

"Due to the short notice, we asked Patrick who the best candidate was. That's you," the manager said.

That was the biggest load of bullshit I'd ever heard in my life. Patrick would never pick me to take over his position. I didn't even know what to say to that, but they didn't care. They just kept talking.

"We will fill everyone in when we send the email, but if anyone asks, please tell them we're looking for a replacement for Mr. Callan as fast as we can. Also, you're going to have to start looking for someone to take your position now that your team is down a person."

I shook my head. They wanted me to be the boss and hire someone. I didn't have the first clue on what to do to hire a replacement.

"Someone from HR will be in touch with you. They'll post your old job soon and give you a list of candidates as early as the end of the week," the CEO said.

"Wait. This is not a step I'm comfortable with."

I might as well have been talking to myself because they ignored me.

"Thanks, Ms. Scott. We'll be in touch soon," Mr. Randu said and hung up the video call.

I sat at Cal's desk for a few seconds, processing everything, but I needed way more than a few minutes to do that. I slowly got up from the chair and left the office in an almost-zombie-like mode.

I didn't want to be the supervisor. I didn't want to be in charge.

And I really, really didn't want Cal to quit.

Everyone was looking up from their computers as I walked past, and I figured they had to be looking at the email the two men had been talking about. When I reached my desk, I dropped into it.

"Cal quit? Patrick's gone? You're our new supervisor?" Leslie said in shock. "What do you think that's all about?"

I shook my head. "I don't know. They didn't tell me. They just said Cal had quit and Patrick was being transferred to Chicago."

"Have you heard from Cal?"

I quickly grabbed my phone from my desk and unlocked it.

Nothing.

"He hasn't texted or called me," I said, alarmed.

"Call him," Leslie suggested.

I dialed his number, but it went to voice mail. "Shit." I went to my messages and sent him a text instead.

> Me: What the hell happened at your meeting today? I just got promoted. Patrick's gone, but they told me you'd quit. Please say it isn't true.

I hung on to my phone like it was my lifeline and went over the video call over and over in my head. There was something the CEO and president hadn't said.

Finally, my phone buzzed.

> Cal: It's true. I put in my notice this morning. I can't talk about it right now. I'll fill you in later. Congratulations on the new position.

I frowned. Cal's text seemed distant and impersonal. Something was definitely up.

> Me: When are you getting back home?

Three dots appeared. And then went away.

They appeared again. And went away again.

I could only think that this meant Cal didn't know what to say to me. That was not good.

> Cal: I need to take care of a few things here.
> I'll let you know when I get back.

That sounded vague, but I didn't want to push. Whatever had happened in Chicago, had to of been bad.

> Me: Okay. Miss you.

> Cal: Miss you too.

At least he hadn't hesitated to send that back to me.

"What did Cal say?" Leslie asked.

I put my phone down on my lap. "Not much. He said he'd tell me later, but he's also not coming back for a few days. It's weird, but I feel like he might be avoiding me."

Leslie looked sympathetic. "Give him time, Indy. Whatever had happened that made him quit his job must have been big. He might need time to process everything. I'm sure he's not avoiding you. He just doesn't know what to say right now."

"Yeah, you're probably right."

She smiled. "Now, remember my great advice when you're doing my yearly review…boss."

I groaned. "I don't want to be the boss."

"If Patrick can do it, you can too." She shrugged. "You never know; you might like it. And if you don't, you can always quit."

"How do you manage to make things that are a big deal not sound so bad?"

She smiled. "It's a gift." She pointed at me. "Remember that, too, when you evaluate me."

THIRTY-EIGHT
CAL

I HAD LIED TO INDY.

I wasn't staying in Chicago, but I had no idea how I was going to tell her that I had failed. Patrick hadn't been fired —he'd most likely received a raise—and he had gotten it by spying on us. Or hiring someone to spy on us.

That was my fault for underestimating the guy. He'd known that I was looking into him. I should have known he'd retaliate and not go down without a fight.

I couldn't tell Indy that the company she loved, the company she had worked for since college, had black-mailed me into choosing between breaking up with her or firing her. Or that she had been promoted out of retaliation.

I already knew it was a job she didn't want, but I didn't want her to quit because she was mad. She could give her new position a chance. I thought she had great potential to be good at it, and even though she didn't think so, there was a possibility she might end up liking it.

I also didn't want her to feel guilty for me having to quit.

I didn't regret choosing her over the company, but I could already see her taking it upon herself as being responsible.

I didn't land back in Minneapolis until almost midnight. I drove home, dropped my bag at the front door, and collapsed into bed. I didn't think I'd sleep a wink, but I underestimated the stress I'd been under all weekend. I fell asleep in my clothes and didn't wake up until morning.

The sunlight streamed through my windows when I opened my eyes, and my bedside clock showed it was after nine in the morning. It was a silent reminder that I no longer had a job.

I rolled onto my back and stared at the ceiling.

Moving back to Minnesota was supposed to be less stressful than New York. Lately, it had been tenser.

I took a deep breath and climbed out of bed. I stripped off my suit and got in the shower. The hot water felt good, and I considered staying there forever, but I needed to do some job-hunting.

After getting dressed, I went straight to my computer. I had applied to more than one company when I first moved to Minneapolis, but it had been a while. I was sure all the open positions had been filled. The good thing about living somewhere like the Twin Cities was, there were a lot of businesses with many positions. If I had to take something that I was overqualified for, I would do it. I didn't want to burn through my savings.

I also wanted to have a new job as soon as possible, so Indy wouldn't have to fear that she'd put me out of work. None of this was her fault, but I was still concerned she would think it was.

My phone buzzed, and I almost didn't pick it up. I didn't

want to lie to Indy again. Thankfully, it wasn't her. It was the stupid dating app, telling me I had a match.

I dropped my head in my hand. I'd almost forgotten about my brother. *Ugh.* One more thing to worry about.

INDY

By Friday, I knew for sure that Cal was avoiding me. He'd been giving me one-worded responses when I texted him. I didn't even know when he'd gotten back into town because he hadn't really answered the question when I asked. Whenever I tried to call him, he wouldn't pick up. He would text me later, saying he was busy, but I didn't buy it. Not every single time.

It was bullshit, and I was sick of it.

After work, I went straight to Cal's house and marched up to the front door. I didn't know if he was home or not because he usually kept his car in the garage. I wasn't going to risk knocking and letting him pretend like he wasn't there, so I used the key he had loaned me to get in since I hadn't returned it.

"Cal," I called out as I flung the door closed. I wanted him to know I meant business.

He walked out of his office, looking a little disheveled. He had on an old pair of jeans and a T-shirt so worn that the letters were starting to fade, and his hair looked like he'd just gotten out of bed.

"Indy?"

"Yeah. Remember me?"

His brow furrowed. "Obviously, I do."

I stomped over to him. "Then, why are you avoiding me?"

"What?" he said like he didn't know what I was talking about, yet I could see the guilt all over his face.

I put my hands on my hips. "Don't play dumb, Cal. You're smarter than that. We both know it."

He sighed as he walked around me and to the couch, collapsing into it. "I might have been putting you off a little."

I pursed my lips. "That's just another way to say avoid." I walked over to him and sat down. "Why? This doesn't seem like you. Do you not want to be with me anymore?"

He laughed at a joke that clearly only he understood and shook his head. "You are so off the mark; you don't even know."

I sat back on the couch. "Actually, I was pretty sure that wasn't the reason."

An eyebrow shot up. "Oh, really?"

"Yeah." I pointed to him. "You don't strike me as the type of guy to beat around the bush."

"Don't be so sure of that."

I poked him in the leg. "What is going on? Why are you *putting me off*? What happened in Chicago?"

Cal ran his hands down his face and dropped his head against the back of the couch. "Nobody was sick."

"Huh?"

"Nobody was sick last Friday. They purposely left me sitting in the waiting room all day."

"Oh." That did not sound good.

"Monday, they pulled me into a conference room."

"With the HR lady, right?"

"Oh, not just her. The CEO was there as well as the president. And then there was Howard Brown."

I did some deep-diving in my brain and came up with nothing. "Who's Howard Brown?"

Cal turned his head to the side toward me. "Patrick's father-in-law."

I gasped. "What? His father-in-law?"

"Yeah. He's on the board."

"You never told me that."

Cal frowned. "I guess I thought you knew."

I shook my head. "Uh...no, I didn't. But that does explain why Polly never fired him."

"Yeah, well, get this...Patrick was there."

"There? There where?" I leaned forward. "Chicago?"

"Yep."

"What the hell?"

"Indy, they weren't meeting me to discuss Patrick. Not like I had thought anyway. It was a trap."

"What happened?"

Cal pinched his nose and squeezed his eyes shut. "I do not want to tell you this."

"Well, now, you have to."

He dropped his hand and gave me a sad smile. "They found out about us."

This had me sitting up. "But you said it was okay that we dated as long as you weren't my immediate supervisor." I gasped again. "Oh my God, that's why they promoted me." I clenched my teeth. "Those assholes. Joke's on them. I don't want the job anyway."

Cal shook his head. "It doesn't matter, Indy. They were going to give you the job whether you wanted it or not."

"I kind of figured that out when they practically hung up on me after I questioned them about giving me the position." I scratched my head. "But they said you quit."

"I did."

"But why?"

"Because of the HR information about immediate supervisors. They said I either had to break up with you or fire you. Joke's on them. I quit," he said, using my own words.

I thought he was trying to make me laugh, but I was not in the mood.

And while I admired the fact that he had basically figured out a way to get around their blackmail, I couldn't help but notice that he had made all the decisions without talking to me first.

"Did they make you choose right then and there what to do about me?"

"No, they gave me until the end of the week."

I crossed my arms over my chest. "So, why didn't you take it?"

He frowned. "Fuck them, Indy. I wasn't going to let them put me in a position like that."

"Don't you think that's something we should have talked about together?" I pointed out.

Cal didn't answer.

I poked him in the chest. "You had no right, making that decision without speaking to me first."

He put his hand over mine. "Indy, I know how much you

love the company. You've worked there since you graduated college. Your best friend works there. I had just started. There was no way in hell I was going to fire you." He leaned in close to me. "And there was *no* way I was going to break up with you."

I yanked my hand away and jumped from my seat. "That's not your decision to make." I gestured between the two of us. "That's something for both of us to decide. Together. As a couple."

Cal shook his head in confusion. "Would you have wanted me to fire you?" He narrowed his eyes. "Or would you have wanted me to break it off with you?"

"On Monday, I would have said no, but today? I'm not so sure."

Cal slowly rose from the couch and stood over me. "What the fuck is that supposed to mean?"

"It means, I don't want to be with someone who makes life decisions for me."

Cal clenched his fists in front of him and made a frustrated sound. "Are you fucking kidding me? You're the main reason I tried to get Patrick fired. I quit my job for you. I've been working all week to find another job before I told you all of this, so you wouldn't feel bad. And now, you're pissed at me? For trying to take care of you?"

I stomped my foot and tightened my own hands. "I don't need you to take care of me. I can take care of myself."

Cal blinked a couple of times and shook his head. He held his hands up and stepped back. "Sorry I ever cared about you then."

"Yeah, same here," I said and marched out of his house, more upset now than when I'd come in.

This was why I had wanted to stop dating alpha males.

They thought they knew what was good for me. But I didn't want someone to take care of me. I wanted a partner.

I got into my car and slammed my door so hard that I thought I'd almost broken my window. I was too pissed to care.

I was about halfway home when the reality of our fight hit me. I might not want an alpha male, but I wanted Cal. I liked him—really liked him—and I wasn't prepared for it to be over.

I went from angry to crying within minutes.

I managed to hit a button on my phone.

"Hello?"

"Le-Leslie?"

"Indy, what's wrong?"

"I think Cal and I just broke up."

"Where are you?"

"Dri-driving home from his house."

"I'll meet you at your house."

She clicked off, and I wiped my tears enough so that I could see the road.

I might have lost Cal, but at least I still had my best friend.

THIRTY-NINE
INDY

LESLIE BROUGHT me ice cream and cookie dough and listened while I told her the whole story about what had happened with Cal. Then, she let me vent while she sat without interrupting.

"Why haven't you said anything?" I asked her.

She patted my hand. "You're not ready for my thoughts. This is your night to be mad. We can talk tomorrow."

"No, I want to hear what you think." The truth was, now that I had voiced all my frustration and rage, I was feeling like I might have overreacted a little.

She lifted her eyebrows in question.

"Tell me," I said.

"Promise not to be mad at me too?"

"I'll try really hard."

She gave me a sharp look.

I nudged her with my foot. "I'm kidding. I won't be mad."

"I know you're upset that Cal made the decision to quit

without talking to you, but what other choice did he have? If you were him, what would you have done?"

I shrugged. Not because I didn't really know, but because Leslie had a point.

"I know how much you like Cal, and if he likes you as much, he wasn't going to break up with you for a job he'd had less than two months. And there was no way he was going to fire you. If I were Cal, I wouldn't stick around for a job that did that to me. He has no loyalty to the company, and they obviously have none for him."

"You bring up some very good arguments."

"I have a question for you." Her tone sounded like I might not like what she had to say.

"Okay," I said hesitantly.

"Say you were the one who had been pulled into the conference room like that—you, Indy, not you as Cal—and you knew you wouldn't break up with him or fire him, so you quit. And then you came back home and told Cal what had happened, only for him to ask you why you'd made the decision without him. How would that make you feel?"

I laughed awkwardly. "Do I have to answer?"

"No, because I can already guess what you'd say."

"My immediate thought was, *I'm an adult. I don't need your permission to make my own decisions.*"

Leslie smiled. "Yeah, I figured." She squeezed my hand. "Now, I'm not saying you shouldn't be mad at him for not talking to you about what happened. You have every right to be angry for the way he avoided you to keep you out of the loop. But I do think you need to cut him some slack about the choice he made on Monday when his hand was forced."

I didn't really want to acknowledge it, but I said, "I think you're right."

Ugh. I had been so mean to Cal.

Leslie tilted her head. "Why did he not tell you all week again?"

"Something like he wanted to find a new job before he told me, so I wouldn't feel bad."

"Do you maybe think one of the reasons you got so upset was because you *do* feel a little guilty?"

I looked down at my hands and put some serious thought into her question. Once again, my best friend was right.

"Definitely. If I had never shared my thoughts about Patrick, Cal would never have tried to fire him, and he would never have had to quit." I pulled my shirt over my face. "Oh my God, it's all my fault."

Leslie pulled my shirt down. "That's not what I was trying to say. It's not all your fault. It's just how everything worked out. Sometimes, shit happens. But this is where you can decide to deal with the shit alone or with the man you love."

My eyes widened. "Love? I never said I loved him."

She shrugged. "You never said you didn't either," she said in a singsong voice.

"Well, if I love Cal, then you love Asher." I pointed a finger at her. "Admit it. He's your boyfriend."

She rolled her eyes. "Fine. He's my boyfriend."

"Ha. I knew it."

She playfully shoved my shoulder. "I don't like you."

"I don't believe you. You love me."

"Fine. I do."

"Almost as much as you love Asher."

Leslie gave me the finger.

Later, as I lay in bed, I stared at my ceiling, wondering what I was going to say to Cal. I couldn't quite tell if we'd only had a fight or if we had broken up on top of our fight.

My phone dinged beside me, and I held my breath as I checked to see if it was Cal.

> Cal: I need you to come over. I want to feel you beside me.

For a second, I couldn't figure out why the text seemed familiar, and then I remembered. It sounded a lot like the text I had sent him the first night. I couldn't stop a smile from spreading across my face.

> Me: Who is this?

> Cal: Cal.

> Cal: Who's this? I'm looking for Indy.

> Me: Wrong number.

My smile turned into a grin.

> Cal: Oh crap. Sorry. I must have gotten the number wrong.

> Me: I'm not. What's your address?

I waited for Cal's next message, wondering what he was going to say to me this time.

But rather than my phone beeping again, my doorbell rang.

I walked from my bedroom without turning on any lights, just in case it wasn't Cal. When I saw his dark head through the window by my door, I threw it open.

"You weren't supposed to come here. I was supposed to go to you."

Cal stepped inside and picked me up. "I couldn't wait. I wanted to see you now."

"How'd you get here so fast? Were you sitting outside my house?"

He set me down and closed the door. "At the risk of sounding like a stalker, yes."

I wrapped my arms around his waist and laid my head on his chest. He smelled and felt so good. "How long were you out there before you messaged me?"

"Five minutes."

"Stalker status cleared. Boyfriend status instated." I pulled back and looked up at him. "Is it okay that I call you that?"

"God, yes. Indy, I've been miserable without you this week. And after you left my house today, I haven't been able to think about anything but our fight." He sighed. "I'm pretty sure I bombed my phone interview."

I winced. "Oh no, I messed that up for you too."

He lifted my chin. "Indy, you didn't mess anything up for me. I'm only trying to show you how much you mean to me." He brushed his lips against mine. "I'd rather live in poverty with you than be rich and alone."

"That's kind of sweet."

Cal lifted his brow. "Kind of?"

I wrapped my arms around his neck. "Baby, no one wants to live in poverty."

"Okay. You can be my sugar mama. I'll stay home and raise the kids."

"Kids?"

"Someday."

I grinned. "Someday," I agreed. I dropped my smile. "I'm sorry I overreacted this afternoon about you quitting your job. I can see how difficult of a position you were in, and I shouldn't have gotten mad at you." I poked him in the chest. "But no more keeping things from me. I want to help you when you are going through something, just like I want you to help me."

He smiled. "I understand. You have a deal."

I narrowed my eyes. "And no lying. I know you didn't want me to worry about your meeting, and that's why you said someone was sick, but I want to know. You can't protect me from everything. And I don't want you to either."

He nodded. "Can I take you to bed now? Because it's been over a week, and I'm dying."

I pretended to be irritated, and I rolled my eyes. "Fine. I guess we can go have sex."

"*Yes.*" Cal threw me over his shoulder. "I am fucking horny."

I laughed as he carried me down to my bedroom.

He tossed me on my bed, and I swore, by the time I got my hair out of my face, he was naked.

"Wow. You really are impatient."

He grabbed my pajama bottoms. "Less talk, more naked."

"Okay, okay."

I stripped off my shirt, and Cal climbed on the bed, over me, and then right inside me.

"Ahh…" he said. "Heaven."

I smiled. "You remember that the next time you think about avoiding me."

He kissed my neck. "I'll remember. I don't want us to ever go through that again."

"Are you saying that because you missed me or because you missed my pussy?"

"Both." He lifted his head and guiltily looked down at me. "I'm sorry."

I laughed. "It's okay. I missed your penis too."

He grinned and kissed my neck again. "How dare you. You're just using me for my dick."

"And maybe because I love you."

Cal stiffened and lifted his head again. "What did you say?"

"I love you."

"God, baby." He kissed me slowly and thoroughly. "I love you too."

My heart skipped a beat out of pure joy. I ran my hands through his hair. "Say it again. This time, while you make love to me."

And that was exactly what Cal did.

FORTY
CAL

I WOKE up from a jab to my side.

"Cal, your phone beeped."

I pulled Indy closer and buried my face in her hair. "I don't care. I'm tired."

My phone beeped again. I knew that tone.

"It's annoying," Indy stated.

With as little moving as possible, I reached behind me on the nightstand and felt around for my phone. "Here," I said, handing it to Indy. "It's the stupid dating app. Maybe you can find my brother."

She snatched it out of my hand. "Ooh, I can't wait to see all the guys who like Callie."

"That's not my name."

"To me it is. It's not only a female version of Cal, but Cal plus Leslie equals Callie. It's perfect."

I groaned but didn't argue any further. I was tired.

"Your phone is locked."

I held up my hand and let her use my finger to unlock it.

I managed to doze a little bit more, hearing Indy laugh

247

or make noises every once in a while, which kept me from falling back asleep all the way.

She made a loud gasp that woke me completely, and I'd had enough.

I really did love the woman, but the night before was the first good night of sleep I'd had in more than a week. And she was ruining it.

That meant she needed a good punishment.

"You're killing me, babe."

"I'm sorry, but—"

I knocked my phone out of her hand, pulled her leg up and over my hip, and slid inside her body.

"Holy crap," she said breathlessly.

I ran my hand up her body, cupping her breast and brushing my thumb over her nipple until she began to rock her hips.

I kissed the back of her neck, sucking on the skin there, as I slid my hand in between her legs, going straight for her clit.

She wrapped a hand behind my neck and dug her claws into my back, and I held her tight around me while I thrust inside her as deep as I could go with the goal of bringing us both to orgasm.

Indy began making little mewling noises, and her clit swelled under my fingers.

She was close, and so was I, so I moved my mouth to her ear and whispered, "I love you."

She was like a firecracker in my arms, exploding. I grinned as I slammed inside her and let my own orgasm take hold of me.

We lay there for a few more minutes, not moving as our

breathing returned to normal. I ran my hands over her again, but this time, it was in a soothing way. I loved feeling her bare skin under my fingertips.

"What was that for?" Indy asked.

"For keeping me awake."

She laughed. "But I had a good reason."

She pulled away from me, and my cock wept as it withdrew from her body. I cupped my hand over him to let him know it would be okay; we weren't going to go that long again without having sex with Indy.

Indy crawled off the bed. "I hope you didn't break your phone."

"It's just a phone."

She found my cell and crawled back onto the bed. She pulled the sheet over her lower half, but her breasts were exposed, and I couldn't help myself from taking a taste.

I was getting hard again, but she pushed me away.

"Cal, I found your brother."

I froze. "What?"

"Yeah, I found him. He changed his username, but he's still on here."

I jerked my phone from her hands. "What a dick." I scooted up further on my bed, so I could lean against the headboard and look at my screen.

Indy was right. There he was—Gallant7487. He really was a dick. Gallant men didn't cheat on their wives.

Indy pulled the sheet over her chest and laid her head on my shoulder. "What are you going to do now?"

"What do you think I should do?"

"If you hit that heart there," she said, pointing to my phone, "it shows you're interested in him. You could do that and then wait to see if he messages you. Or you could message him right away."

I looked down on her. "What did you do?"

She turned her eyes toward me. "He liked me and messaged me. I didn't find him. He found me."

I smiled. "For some reason, that makes me feel good."

She bit her bottom lip. "Does it bother you that the first night I texted you, it was meant for your brother?"

"To be honest, I've tried not to think about it."

"To be honest, I was hoping you hadn't been either." She lifted her head. "I want you to know that I have a hundred times more chemistry with you than I did with him. I really did text him that because Leslie had encouraged me to. And because I hadn't had sex in a very long time. You could say, I wasn't being very picky."

I raised my brow. "Hmm…so you're saying you were desperate when you had sex with me." I was teasing her a little, but I also wanted to know how she truly felt.

"*Desperate* is too strong of a word, but you have to remember, you were a stranger." She peeked at me from the corner of her eye. "Do you think less of me now?"

I put my arm around her neck and pulled her close to me. "I don't think less of you. I am a little jealous that my brother was the guy you sent that text to—I can't lie about that—but if you hadn't sent it, we wouldn't have gotten together."

"But then you would still have your job."

I lifted her chin and kissed her. "I think I already said this last night, but in case you forgot, I'd rather be jobless with you."

"You said something like that." She smiled. "I'm your sugar mama, remember?"

I laughed. "Not for long. I have a couple more interviews lined up next week."

"You could have led with that."

I laughed again. "Sorry, baby."

She rubbed her nose against my neck. "I'm so glad you're here with me."

"Me too, Indy. Me too."

She poked my phone screen. "Now, you need to figure out what you're going to do about your brother."

My screen had long gone dark, so I unlocked my phone again and hit the heart button. I'd wait and see what he said to me.

FORTY-ONE
INDY

MONDAY, I went to work with determination flowing through my veins, and the first thing I did was pull up my work email.

Dear Mr. Malone and Mr. Randu,

Thank you for the opportunity to broaden my horizons and expand my skills, but after giving my new position a week, I have decided that being supervisor is not in the best interest for the company. Being a supervisor is more paperwork and less software work, which is my area of expertise. This is where my skills excel, and you would be missing out on my services in making me supervisor.

I understand the company is in a tight spot, having lost two employees at once, so I will help with the position until a new person is hired or promoted.

If this is unacceptable to you, then you may consider this my two weeks' notice.

Thank you for your time.

Lucinda Scott

I hovered my mouse over the Send button as I reread my

email five times. I was nervous about sending it, but I asked myself, *What's the worst that could happen?*

They'd let me go, and I'd have to find a new job. That was it. I'd still have my health. I'd still have my family and my best friend. And I'd still have Cal.

I closed my eyes and hit the left button on my mouse.

"Uh…what are you doing?" Leslie said as she came up behind me.

Now that I had decided to send my email and step down, I was sitting at *my* desk again.

I looked over my shoulder at her, watching as she put her stuff away in her desk. "Sending an email to the CEO and president. I also CC'd the HR lady who was a part of Cal's meeting. I told them I don't want the supervisor position, and that if they couldn't accept that, then I was putting in my two weeks' notice."

"Good for you."

"Yeah, it looks like we might be roommates again."

Leslie and I had lived together in college and a few years after.

She shook her finger at me. "You can move in with Cal because I'm already getting a new roommate."

"You are?" I narrowed my eyes, imagining another woman moving in with my best friend and having this stranger slowly replace me. "Who is she?"

Leslie laughed. "Not *she*." She reached over and patted my hand. "You're still my bestie." She turned her eyes down, looking almost shy. "It's Asher."

I gasped and clapped my hands together. "Really?" I jumped up from my chair and hugged her. "I'm so happy for you."

"Yeah, yeah, let's not make a big deal of it."

I let her go and sat back down in my chair. "Okay, I won't make a big deal."

"Then, why are you still grinning?"

I lifted my shoulders in glee. "Because I'm thrilled for you."

She laughed. "You're a goofball."

"You can insult me all you want. I'm too happy for your words to hurt me."

My computer pinged, and I looked at my screen. My face fell.

"What's wrong?"

"They emailed me back. Already."

"Good mood ruined," Leslie joked dryly. "Might as well open it and get it over with. But, Indy?"

I looked at her.

"No matter what happens, if you really did lose your job and need a place to live, you know you're more than welcome to stay with me."

"Thanks, babe."

She nodded her head toward the computer. "Now, read it. No time like the present."

I took a deep breath and opened the email from the CEO.

Dear Ms. Scott,

Thank you for giving the supervisory position a fair attempt. Since this was a position you had not applied for, we accept your notice.

I looked away and started sweating. When I'd sent the email, I hadn't really thought they'd let me quit. They had to know what info I had on them. If I wanted to, I could publicize it.

Leslie elbowed me. "Hey, it worked."

I hadn't realized she was reading over my shoulder. "Huh?"

"They aren't going to force you to be the supervisor and are letting you go back to your old job once they hire someone."

I quickly finished reading the entire message.

We have already posted the supervisor position. Once it is filled, you may return to your original position.

Thank you for helping the company in our time of need.

Sincerely,

Mr. Malone

A wave of relief went through my body, and I slumped in relief. "I won."

"You sure did," Leslie said. "They know you have dirt on them. You just made them your bitch."

I laughed. "I don't know about that, but it's a fun thought. I'm just relieved to be able to stay at a job I like with my best friend."

FORTY-TWO

CAL

I DRUMMED my fingers against the table as I waited for my brother to show up at the restaurant. After LovelyLady555 —or Callie, as Indy liked to call my profile—had hearted my brother, he had messaged two days later.

Flirting with my brother was one of the most horrible things I had ever done, and I usually had to hand the phone over to Indy to finish. But it had worked because he asked me out.

I didn't want my brother to claim entrapment even though I wasn't the police, so after I made myself known, I'd let him make all the moves.

Joel showed up right on time, and I watched him speak to the hostess and get a table before I approached him.

I took a deep breath and walked over. "Mind if I sit?"

My brother peered up at me, and his eyes grew wide. He scanned the room in a panic.

"Don't worry. LovelyLady555 isn't going to show up."

"What—how—what are you talking about?"

I pulled out the chair across from Joel and sat. "Lovely-Lady555 isn't coming because I'm LovelyLady555."

My brother swallowed, looking like a deer caught in headlights.

"What are you doing, man? You have a wonderful wife at home, taking care of your kid, and you're on dating sites, searching for women."

"I don't do anything with them. I just go on dates." He held up his hands. "I swear I've never done more than peck."

"Yeah, that's what Indy said."

"She told you?"

"Of course she told me. She's my girlfriend. How do you think I found you, dumbass?"

He turned his head away. "I was thinking since you hadn't said anything after dinner at Mom and Dad's, she hadn't told you."

"Yeah, well, you're wrong." I sighed. "I'm going to ask again. What the hell are you doing?"

He shrugged. "I don't know, okay? I feel smothered at home. Dana got pregnant, so we got married, and suddenly, I have a wife and kid."

Joel was younger than me by eight years, but he'd been in his late twenties when he got married and they had Oliver. He hadn't exactly been a teenager.

"So, you get a divorce. You don't cheat on her."

Joel looked down at his hands. "I know; I know. But it turns out, I love Oliver, more than I ever thought possible." He turned his eyes up at me. "I couldn't bear it if Dana took him away from me."

"She wouldn't do that—unless maybe she catches you

cheating on her and does it out of revenge. Still, I can't see that. She doesn't strike me as that type of person."

He fingered the napkin in front of him. "You might be right." He met my eyes. "What do I do now?"

"You delete your account on that app, and you remove it from your phone. You find a good therapist for yourself and work things out in your head. Then, you come clean to your wife about everything. Your worries, your feelings of being trapped, and your cheating."

My brother opened his mouth. I stopped him with the rise of my hand.

"I don't care if there wasn't sex. It was cheating, and Dana is going to be hurt."

My brother's shoulders fell, and I knew he knew I was right.

"Then, if Dana still wants to work on things, you two go to counseling together."

"That seems like a lot of work."

"No shit, Sherlock. Relationships are hard work. But you owe it to your wife."

Joel slowly nodded. "You're right."

"Now, take out your phone and do the first part."

He sneered as he pulled out his phone. "You sure are bossy."

"Yeah, that's what big brothers do."

I watched Joel pull up the app. "I should have known it was you," he said, shooting me a look. "The name Callie should have given you away."

I frowned. "I never told you my name was—" I closed my eyes and shook my head. "Indy." *That little turd*. I did have to smile at the thought though. *Man, I love that woman.*

"She helped you?" he asked, alarmed.

"Yes. We don't keep secrets from each other." *Now*. After the whole job debacle. But Joel didn't need to know that.

My brother deleted the app completely from his phone and waved it at me. "There. Are you happy now?"

"Not yet. Come talk to me in a few months—after you've followed the rest of my advice."

My brother took a deep breath. "Fine."

"Joel?"

"Yeah."

"No matter what, you're still my little bro, and I kind of, sort of love you. I know this is going to be hard, so if you ever want to talk, call me, okay?"

Joel smiled. "Kind of, sort of?"

"Yeah." That was all he was getting from me.

"I kind of, sort of love you too, man. And thank you for helping me out and not telling Mom and Dad."

"The thought had crossed my mind, but I wanted to give you the chance to fix your own mistakes first."

"Thanks. And I will. I promise."

EPILOGUE

INDY

"TO ONE YEAR," I said, clinking my glass against Cal's.

It had been one year since the night I texted Cal and asked him to come over, and we were at dinner, celebrating.

"To one year," he said with a smile.

We each took a sip of our champagne and set our glasses down.

"I hope the server gets here soon. I'm starving."

Cal laughed at me and picked up his phone.

"Cal, you promised no work tonight."

Cal hadn't bombed the interview he'd done all those months ago. He had gotten a second interview in person and ended up getting the job. Unfortunately, it was more demanding than his last position, and sometimes, he had to take calls and do work outside of business hours.

"Sorry, honey, but this is really important."

My phone vibrated in my purse, and I figured if he was on his phone, I could be on mine too.

I pulled it out and looked at my screen. It was a text from Cal.

My eyes flew up to him, but he was still staring down at his own phone.

> Cal: I need you to come over. I want you to move in with me and be my wife.

I gasped, and tears filled my eyes. I glanced up at him.

He was staring at me with a box in his hand. He put it on the table and pushed it over to me.

I looked back down.

> Me: Who is this?

I lifted my eyes enough to see Cal smirk.

> Cal: The man of your dreams.

> Me: Sorry. The man of my dreams is sitting right across from me.

I set my phone down and picked up the ring. It was a beautiful diamond solitaire that I had commented on in passing one day when we were shopping at the mall. He'd remembered.

I started crying out of joy. I was going to be Cal's wife.

He took my hand in his. "Does this mean yes or no?"

I laughed through my tears and nodded. "Yes."

He grinned at me. "I love you."

"I love you too."

He picked up the box. "Now, let me put the ring on you."

I held up my pointer finger. "Just one second. This other

guy also asked me to marry him tonight. I have to go tell him he has the wrong number."

MY FAVORITE MISTAKE SAMPLE

MADELINE

I watched my boyfriend, Harris, pull a suit from his closet and frown.

"Did you hear what I said?" I asked from my seat on the end of his bed.

Harris walked over and laid his clothes over his traveling garment bag without taking a single glance in my direction.

"Harris?"

He looked up at me, startled, almost as if he'd forgotten I was even there.

Sadly, this had been the state of our relationship lately.

"What?" he asked.

"Friday night."

"What about Friday night?"

I ground my teeth together as I stopped myself from reaching over and strangling him. "My friends want to get together for my birthday."

I watched a variety of emotions cross Harris's face. In

the year and a half we'd been dating, he'd never hidden the fact that he didn't care for my friends, and I sat and waited for him to make up an excuse as to why we couldn't go.

Harris pursed his lips. "Why don't you and I go out to dinner on Friday instead?" He smiled at me, giving me one hundred percent of the Harris Starling charm. It was the Harris smile that had gotten me to go on a date with him. And it was the Harris smile that had gotten me to sleep with him.

But now, it did nothing for me.

I mentally rolled my eyes because I was not some business deal he had to make. And I didn't answer right away because I didn't want to say something snarky I'd regret.

I picked up my phone and texted my best friend, Griffin.

> Me: Guess what.

Griffin: You won the lottery.

> Me: Ha! I wish. No. I called it. Harris is trying to convince me to ditch you guys on Friday and go to dinner with him alone.

Griffin: Fucking prick. And you didn't call it. I did.

> Me: Technically, we both did.

Griffin: What did you tell him?

I looked up from my phone to see Harris had moved over to his dresser and was pulling out socks and underwear. I hated his tighty-whities. I never found them attractive.

Boxers or boxer briefs were better.

Commando was the best.

My phone buzzed in my hand.

> Griffin: You still there? What did he say?

"We're going to dinner on Saturday night," I reminded Harris.

He paused and turned around. "Hmm?"

I sighed. "We're having dinner on Saturday, remember? That's why I wanted to go out with my friends on Friday." My tone had gone from casual to firm as I had to remind him of our plans once again. This was not the first time he'd forgotten.

Guilt flooded Harris's face, and his brown eyes avoided mine.

"What?" I asked with full-on irritation now. I knew him well enough to know that whatever he was going to say, I wasn't going to like it.

"I'm leaving town."

I lifted an eyebrow and looked at his clothes and luggage strewn about his bed. "I know."

"No, I mean, I'm leaving on Saturday now instead of Sunday."

"It's Wednesday, and you're just telling me this now?"

He shrugged. *Shrugged.*

"You do realize, my birthday is on Friday? A birthday you promised to be in town for." It wasn't every day that your girlfriend turned thirty.

Harris's blond brow furrowed. "I thought your birthday was on Saturday."

I dropped my face in my hand and rubbed my forehead. I was so tired.

My phone vibrated in my other hand, so I peeked at it.

Griffin: Dump his ass.

Keeping my head down, I shot back a quick message.

Me: You don't even know what he said.

Griffin: It wasn't good if you're not even telling me what he said.

Me: You're right. He doesn't even know what day my birthday is.

Griffin: Break it off. You deserve better. Besides, you're always whining about not getting any.

I chuckled. Griffin always had a way of making me smile.

And that was why he was my best friend.

Me: I don't whine.

But Griffin was right. Harris and I hadn't had sex in weeks. We hadn't had decent sex in months. And unfortunately, we'd *never* had great sex.

Maybe I did complain a lot. I would never admit to whining though.

"What's so funny?"

I looked up at Harris, standing there with his hand on his hip, judgment on his face.

He probably had a good guess as to who I was texting, and I was sure he didn't like it.

Griffin and Harris had never gotten along.

I lost all humor as I stood and looked Harris in the eyes. It wasn't hard, as he was only two inches taller than me.

"Don't worry about dinner on Friday or Saturday."

Harris cocked his head. "I don't understand."

"We're not going to dinner either night."

"Don't you want your birthday present?"

"From you?" I said as I headed for the bedroom door. "No."

I heard the dresser drawer close behind me and the click of Harris's dress shoes on his hardwood floor as he followed.

Thank God it'd never become *my* hardwood floor.

Harris had asked me to move in more than once, but I always had a reason to say no.

Now, I knew the reason was gut instinct.

"Madeline, I don't understand."

I grabbed my jacket and purse from the couch on my way to the front door without answering right away.

The man was undeniably clueless.

I yanked open the thick oak door and turned around as the cool autumn air hit my back. "I don't need your birthday present because I am giving myself the best one."

He frowned. "And what's that?"

I grinned. "I am getting rid of you."

"What?"

"It's over, Harris. I'm done."

A thousand pounds fell from my shoulders, and I felt freer than I had in months.

I turned toward the outside air and sucked in a deep breath before pulling on my coat.

Damn, it felt good.

"You can't break up with me."

I looked over my shoulder at Harris. "I just did. Have fun on your business trip. Please don't call me when you get back."

I stepped out onto the front stoop and closed the door behind me. "Good riddance," I muttered. I hit a button on my phone and lifted it to my ear.

"You got Griffin," a deep rasp said in my ear.

Hearing his voice made me realize I had made the absolute best decision. My bestie was going to be so proud of me.

"Hey."

"Hey. I was wondering if I was ever going to hear back from you."

"I did it."

"Did what?"

"I broke up with Harris."

Griffin laughed in disbelief. "You're shitting me."

I smiled at the sound of hope in his voice as I unlocked my car and got behind the wheel. "I'm serious."

"*About fucking time*," Griffin said a little too loudly in my ear, and I pulled the phone back with a grin.

I heard his big boots hit the floor and then the creak of his office door opening. I pictured him walking the hallway to the main room of his bar.

"She dumped his ass," Griffin shouted to the room, and I heard a bunch of cheers erupt. He put the receiver back to his mouth and said, "Hear that? Everyone's excited for you."

Griffin had worked hard on opening his bar, and he had a steady stream of regulars who liked to hang out almost every night. They all knew about my boyfriend and how Griffin didn't like the guy.

I grinned. "Yeah, I heard."

"They all want you to come in, so they can buy you a drink," he told me.

I didn't know if that was true, but I didn't care. I could use one right about now. "I'll be there in ten minutes."

"See ya then, Mads."

———————

Get My Favorite Mistake now!

ABOUT THE AUTHOR

R.L. Kenderson is two best friends writing under one name.

Renae has always loved reading, and in third grade, she wrote her first poem where she learned she might have a knack for this writing thing. Lara remembers sneaking her grandmother's Harlequin novels when she was probably too young to be reading them, and since then, she knew she wanted to write her own.

When they met in college, they bonded over their love of reading and the TV show *Charmed*. What really spiced up their friendship was when Lara introduced Renae to romance novels. When they discovered their first vampire romance, they knew there would always be a special place in their hearts for paranormal romance. After being unable to find certain storylines and characteristics they wanted to read about in the hundreds of books they consumed, they decided to write their own.

One lives in the Minneapolis-St. Paul area and the other in the Kansas City area where they both work in the medical field during the day and a sexy author by night. They communicate through phone, email, and whole lot of messaging.

You can find them at http://www.rlkenderson.com, Facebook, Instagram, TikTok, and Goodreads. Join their

reader group! Or you can email them at rlkenderson@
rlkenderson.com, or sign up for their newsletter. They
always love hearing from their readers.

Made in the USA
Coppell, TX
25 February 2024

29420348R00154